THE WANDERERS

PART ONE

A TRAIL TO SOMEWHERE

REBECCA KEEFE

Inquiries and Book Orders
should be addressed to:

Great Writers Media
Email: info@greatwritersmedia.com
Phone: 877-600-5469

ISBN: 978-1-960939-08-1 (sc)
ISBN: 978-1-960939-09-8 (ebk)

Historical References

All locations in this book are fictitious with the exception of the following:

Rosedale, Mississippi; Oxford, Mississippi; Memphis, Tennessee; Atlanta, Georgia; St. Louis; Independence; and St. Joseph, Missouri.

* * *

The battle at Round Mountain in Oklahoma territory is one of the first Civil War battles fought in the Indian Territory. The name refers to several hills that lay north of the Cimmaron River in southeastern Pawnee County.

Oklahoma Historical Society (www.okhistory.org/publications/enc.pnp?En-

try=RO035) also, https://en.wikipedia.
org/wiki/Battle_of_Round_Mountain

* * *

The town of Oxford Mississippi was established in 1937 on fifty acres which had once
belonged to the Choctaw Indians. This land
was presented to the county by John Chisholm,
John J. Craig, and John D. Martin, who had
purchased the land from the Indians. (visitox-
fordms.com/about-oxford/history/)

In my book, I took a little writers license and
fictionalized Emiel LeClair and his part in this
endeavor.

* * *

All biblical references are based on King James
Version, Holy Bible, Thomas Nelson Edition.

Prologue

While the American Civil War wreaked havoc on the geographic landscape of this country, it also scarred the souls of its people, inflicting a loss that far exceeded the outcome of which side celebrated victory. This loss, intensified by death, the destruction of families, demise of wealth, and homeland created for many a desperate insecurity that propelled them on a quest for a new life. They weren't exactly sure where they'd find it, but all roads pointed west, where there was hope and opportunity. Some sought a new start, even adventure, while others adopted a new sense of self. However, others still pursued vengeance to assuage their wounded spirits. So, sustained by their faith in God, a determination to survive, or their vengeful obsession, many rich, poor, young, old, and unfortunately, degenerate reprobates went searching. I call these individuals 'The Wanderers'.

Chapter One

Traders Bluff, Mississippi, April 1, 1866

Glaring furiously at the body that was now sprawled, face down on the bare wooden floor amidst a sprinkling of ashes, empty whiskey bottles, and overturned furniture, the tall, thin girl stood stiffly poised as though waiting. Her gaze slowly examined the length of the man, searching for any sign of life; a twitch or even a moan, but as far she could tell, he appeared to be dead. *No movement, no breathing, nothing.* She glanced at the iron poker that she clenched tightly in her upraised hands; its pointed end glistened red with the results of her mindless reaction. Had she killed him? She wasn't sure, but one thing was certain, Hiram Walters was never going to hurt her again.

As Hannah Todd continued to watch the inert body of her *so-called* stepfather, the anger that had fueled this rare act of retaliation, gave way to a trembling fear, rendering movement impossible. She watched the blood from the wound on his head pool on the floor, she gasped loudly to retrieve the much-needed breath she'd been holding. Immediately, the consequences of her actions came to mind and her mind screamed it was time to run, to get out before the others came back. Time, the one thing she always had in abundance, was now fleeing quickly as its passage echoed loudly from the tick-tock of the old clock on the mantle.

Hannah slowly lowered her arms, releasing her white knuckled grip of the weapon just enough to fling the bloody thing into the fireplace. Looking around bemusedly, her thoughts were a jumbled riot of what to do next; and it was certainly not clean this up. Wiping sweaty hands down her pants, she took her first step, faltering, then more firm step towards a life on the run.

"Hiram's gang will be back soon," she whispered glancing anxiously towards the door, "and that pack of cutthroats will string me up for sure after carrying out their depraved ideas of 'what females are really for'," she shuddered.

Moving hurriedly, she stumbled over his booted foot. She reached out wildly for something to prevent a fall, she managed to grab the mantle and right her balance before joining Hiram on the floor.

"Slow down," she muttered, taking a moment to breathe and peer closely at the body for signs indicating he might be coming round.

Releasing a low uneasy snort, she quickly jerked her foot off the offending limb. No wonder it didn't rouse him, she had stepped on his wooden leg. Sweat trickled down her back, stinging raw fresh welts left from an early morning scourging that occurred before sunrise. Hiram had found her asleep face-down, leaving her back a vulnerable target. The deep gashes cut by the whip had fallen across partially healed scabs left from a previous onslaught.

He'd always been abusive, taking advantage of his greater size and strength to bully her in line. A doubled-up fist and booted foot were often applied, but as she got older, his weapon of choice was a braided leather whip. These bouts of so-called discipline would end with a threat that made it clear that retribution would be doubly worse if she tried to run away. Hannah had tried only once, and the reprisals had been far worse than anything he'd ever threatened.

Lately, he seemed to be pushing her to try again as every time her back was turned, he inflicted injury along with vile curses labeling her the lowest form among females. She had taken all of it shamefully, until today. Images of her deceased mother cowering and begging Hiram not to strike again crowded her thoughts, reminding Hannah how he'd destroyed that fragile woman. Well, that wasn't going to be her fate! Today, the gang wasn't here to back him up and when he attacked for a second time, she'd fought back instead of her usual cringing efforts to evade the onslaught and flee to the woods out back.

"*Move, run. Get out now,*" her frantic mind urged, but still she continued to relive the last hour.

Hiram hadn't been anywhere close when she'd bent down to tidy up the fireplace, but as earlier, he'd caught her unaware. She figured her mind snapped when that first lash curled across her back, inflicting an agony that must have addled her senses, because she couldn't recall a single tangible thought that prompted her to fight back. She simply reacted, and without thinking, curled her hand around that poker with a grip so fierce it hurt, before springing up to confront a startled Hiram. His panicked expression inspired a dogged resolution that today things would turn out differently. Hannah Todd had taken her last beating.

That feeling of vindication still pulsed through her body as she recalled the flash of fear that replaced his gloating expression, prompting him to drop the whip to shield his face. How many times had he incited that same desperate fear in her? Shaking her head slowly, she relived that first strike across his jaw, leaving a long gash, how he'd twisted and stumbled back to fall to the floor landing on all fours. Then she'd struck again; using both arms and committing all her strength and five years of pent-up anger to deliver a final vicious blow to the back of his head.

Hannah shrugged off some emerging misgivings, refusing to be ashamed of her actions. While she'd never reacted so defiantly before, in all honesty she'd longed to, many times, not only to Hiram but his partner Cutler as well. The old clock suddenly chimed one, its reverberating bong caused Hannah to jerk spasmodically as reality intruded.

Moving cautiously, she crossed to the back corner of the room where a curtained off area concealed a bed crudely constructed from various pieces of tree stumps and crates. Some of the crates had been left intact making them handy for storing things. In one of the storages, she retrieved a faded carpetbag. The fear of someone coming, or Hiram getting back to his senses before she could get away was palpable, causing her hands to tremble and clumsily drop the bag before finally wrenching it open.

It was an old but sturdy container and would easily hold her meager possessions of two shirts, a skirt, and another pair of pants; all procured from one of Hiram's raids. She gathered her mother's silver backed brush and comb along with a faded photograph of her parents and stowed theme among the clothing. She tossed the last things left which were some cleaning cloths and a bar of lavender soap that was so old it hardly has its scent anymore.

Catching sight of a long-forgotten item, she halted before sliding the makeshift drawer back under the bed. Momentarily, she was transported to another time when life was gentle and filled with James Todd's smiling approval and Irene's tea parties. She reached down to pick up a pair of old tea gloves, recalling her mother's stern reminder, "*A true lady is never seen in public without gloves.*"

"Oh poppa," Hannah whispered quietly, "I wish you were here."

She tossed the gloves, along with her memories in the bag, pushing away thoughts of melancholy. Time for that would come tomorrow or the next day or some other hour when her chance for freedom wasn't in jeopardy.

"Mustn't forget my gun," she whispered.

Scooting the leg of the bed over, she reached to pull up a loose board from the floor to retrieve the .44 Colt Pistol that had belonged to her father. She kept it hidden from Hiram, along with a few remaining bullets. Replacing the board, she moved the bed back and just for reassurance spun the cylinder to make sure the gun was fully loaded. Counting four remaining bullets, she realized that from here on out every shot must be fired only if necessary and above all, be accurate. Rising quickly, she laid the gun and cartridges on top of the packed clothing.

Food would be the next order of business, but she took one step and stopped abruptly. The prospect of walking past Hiram's outstretched arm was almost her undoing, but no… she will not cower. So, she leaned forward to peak around the curtain to make sure he still lay where he'd fallen. Biting her lips nervously, she stared intently at the seemingly lifeless body, watching for some movement, but nothing happened.

However, familiar with his sneaky ways, she took out the revolver and cocked it just in case he was lying in wait to grab her. Today's actions would demand more than a warning threat. She might actually have to put a bullet in his heart. With shaking hands, she aimed the weapon between the man's shoulders and while keeping a watchful eye alert for any change, reached to grab the long shoulder strap someone had attached to the old satchel and stepped determinedly around the curtain.

Spying Hiram's Henry repeating rifle, she knew it would be fully loaded and come in handy for more than just putting food in her belly, so skirting the edges of the room, she snatched up which was the rifle and headed to the cooking area. She refused to call it a kitchen. A kitchen was like the one in her home back in Oxford with a real cook stove and ovens; not some designated part of a room that presented a wood stove, rickety cupboard, and a rough worktable.

Hannah suddenly froze in mid step, afraid to move. Was that a gasp? Listening anxiously for several minutes, she finally turned to watch the still motionless body, but nothing had changed; must've been her imagination. Grateful for the reprieve, she hurried to the cupboard, grabbed an empty flour sack and filled it with a sheathed hunting knife that belonged to one of the gang members, and the last few cans of beans and peaches that lined the shelves. Lastly, a box of matches and some biscuits and rabbit meat left from breakfast were tossed in the bag before she slipped out the backdoor, carefully closing it without a slam.

Heading quickly toward the barn, she was almost overcome by a paralyzing fear of Hiram being really dead, or the fear of getting caught by Cutler. She took several stumbling steps over these thoughts before stopping to take a deep breath.

"Calm down, there's no time for panic. I've done nothing but defend myself," she stated emphatically.

It had simply come down to her life or his or theirs, if the gang chose to come after her which they would.

Entering the barn Hannah saw that Hiram's horse, Samson, has the only mount available. This was almost enough to make her start out on foot. Samson, a high-strung thoroughbred, had a reputation for orneriness that alternated between sweet natured compliance and out right meanness, unless you were Hiram. Just the thought of getting on this horse was daunting, especially for someone with her lack of riding experience. She knew how but had been barred from riding any one's mount, except Pinkies, and only then in the presence of Cutler or one of the others.

Needless to say, it wasn't an outing she often took advantage of.

Samson was now the only asset left of the Todd fortune Hiram had married into and run through. Actually, the animal appeared to be the only possession among all the vast estate he ever cared for. He'd treated her mother and her like dirt once the marriage vows were said, selling off anything of value in their Oxford plantation and then letting the taxes accumulate until they were forced out. However, he knew good horseflesh and Samson had proved his value as a fast and surefooted getaway many times as the gang sped away from robberies, raids, and the law.

Looking around for tack, Hannah recalled the last time she'd been in this part of the barn was to help her mother bury two items, items she'd almost forgotten. Hopefully, they were still where Irene had buried them. Glancing from one corner of the building to the other, uncertain where the exact spot was, she approached the barn's left back corner and began pushing aside a variety of animal hides along with a jumble of other stolen items; clothing, hats, even some tarnished silverware that spilled out of an old saddle blanket.

"No telling who all these things had belonged to," she muttered; heedless of the mess, her search was making.

"Finally," she let out a sigh of relief, while unearthing a marked pelt, along with a bout of coughing and sneezing as a cloud of stale odor and dust swirled upward.

Hannah shoved aside the hides, pilfered pilfered booty, and earthen debris to reveal a rolled up old Aubusson carpet. Unrolling this, she lifted out her mother's wedding dress from her first marriage and with shaking hands, she quickly began folding it down to fit in the carpetbag. There was an oddity about the dress. It felt heavy and had small, tufted buttons in unusual places, but there wasn't time to investigate now.

She tucked it under the other packed items in the carpet bag and reached for a large cedar box that had been hidden in the folds of the dress. This contained her mother's jewelry; elaborate lavish pieces handed down from French royalty through each generation of LeClaire brides. Hiram had badgered Irene relentlessly concerning the whereabouts of these jewels, but finally gave up after being convinced the housemaid had stolen them before running off.

Hannah remembered watching her mother bury these things during Hiram's first raiding trip away after abandoning them in what Irene called *"the devil's wasteland for nobodies"* in other words she explained,

"If you found yourself dumped in such a place as Traders Bluff, you had no connections and no worth to anyone. You either joined in his nefarious works or you're nothing to him… you're nobody."

She'd worked tirelessly moving things and digging underneath them while issuing Hannah a stern warning to never let anyone know of their whereabouts.

"This is for your future," she implored. "Hiram destroyed your inheritance… the future you should have had, and for that, I'm sorry. This is all I have left now… and it's yours," she'd cried vehemently. "Don't ever let him know where these are. In fact, never come to this spot unless you're leaving here for the last time. And never let on that you had an inkling of where they were hidden if someone should find them. He'd probably kill you over that."

Her mother's rant ended with one last vicious statement, "I'd rather they rust in the dirt than for that worthless piece of trash to get them."

Opening the box, Hannah looked down on an assortment of colorful jewels and wished there was time to examine these treasures. Other than her mother's wedding rings, earrings, and necklace, she'd never seen any of these pieces. They sure looked pretty and sparkling even in the dim light of the barn.

"Hopefully, they will secure my future," she spoke quietly, dumping it all in a large hidden pocket inside her bag.

Pushing the box back to its hiding place, she started to cover it, but changed her mind. There just wasn't time. Instead, she hurriedly saddled Samson, talking in low soothing tones to cover her nervousness. She secured a bed role, a rain slicker, and her carpetbag behind the saddle; then tied the food and an empty canteen to the saddle's pommel. At last, she filled a feed bag with oats.

"Now, how long do you think these will last," she asked the horse while hanging them beneath the saddle boot she'd slipped the rifle into.

Casting a last quick glance back at the house, Hannah was assured that nothing looked amiss. In fact, it all appeared normal, wood waiting to be chopped, clothes hanging on the line, nothing out of place. She stared at the cabin door, expecting Hiram to come stumbling out waving his whip cursing to high heaven. When that didn't happen, she released a sigh of relief and turned to lead Samson out the back of the barn.

"The journey begins here… please be good for me," she begged the animal, before grabbing a piece of brush to sweep away their tracks.

She chose to lead Samson until they were further away; aware that a horse and rider left deeper impressions in the ground, making tracking easier. Thankfully, the moccasins she was wearing left little to no track at all behind a skinny person like her. Setting a zigzag path through the thick woods, Hannah led Samson towards the same creek she carried water from every day, only this time staying far off the well-trod path. Thinking frantically, she decided they'd wade down the stream past the old Hinton Homestead. This would allow them a couple of hours of untraceable getaway.

Leafy limbs slapped her face as she rapidly pushed through thick blackberry brambles and tall bamboo thickets while watching carefully for snakes or mole holes to stumble on. She was also on the lookout for hunters, or worse other good-for-nothings who had committed a foul deed in Traders Bluff and was now hiding from some other villain they'd cheated on or half killed; after all, crooks were about the only kind of people you'd find in this part of the country.

Traders Bluff, a lawless community about twenty miles north of the river town of Rosedale, Mississippi thrived despite its depraved occupants that somehow managed to remain unnoticed and therefore unrestrained by lawmen. Once in a while, a band of men would ride through in pursuit of some unlucky offender, but this had become a rarity especially since the war ended. Even the blue bellies, that ruthlessly patrolled the South, overlooked them. Because of this, the small hamlet comprised of four ramshackle taverns, a mercantile, a seedy boarding house, and a livery with blacksmith had become a harbinger for river pirates, gunslingers, draft dodgers, and other degenerate leftovers from the war. There was no law, no jail, and if anyone had dared try to establish these, they'd find themselves run out of town or lynched.

The only other business in town was a doctor who stayed drunk most of the time and gambled the rest. Judging from his appearance, he looked to be as old as a century but despite his looks, many outlaws swore that when he was sober you'd be hard pressed to find a better saw bone.

Hannah splashed into the creek, shivering as the cold water rose to cover her about mid-thigh. At least its clearness would allow her to see where she was stepping. Noting familiar landmarks, she watched and listened for anything out of place. Trees were spreading new growth, buttercups bloomed along the bank, birds dipped and scurried to build nest; it seemed that everything was eager to pursue new life.

Despite marauders that might be lurking about, Hannah felt safer in these woods then she had ever been in Hiram's cabin. Over the years, she had hunted them for any source of food to be found, nuts, wild greens, and especially game. Because of this, several of the old trails that crisscrossed the creek and surrounding area were familiar territory. She'd heard the gang talk about escape plans and how some of these trails led to the river, which was a good reason to come this way instead of heading toward Traders Bluff.

A loud crash and snap from the creek bank broke the silence, causing Hannah to stop and halting Samson with a firm hand. Abruptly, a huge buck bounded through the trees, pulling up shortly at the edge of the stream. He posed there, nostrils flaring, head erect, warily surveying the area. Hannah stood as still as possible, hardly daring to breathe.

She kept to the horse's side to remain less visible, while slowly pulling the rifle from its scabbard, just in case. If the deer stopped to drink everything was okay, but if he continued across the stream, then something or someone was after him, which could lead to danger. Warily she scanned the trees and bushes behind the deer, peering anxiously through their thick maze.

"Finally," she whispered in relief as the animal lowered its large head and began drinking water.

Hannah decided to keep the rifle in hand and recognized even more the urgency to hurry if she was going to put any meaningful distance between her and the cabin. As the deer ambled away, she mounted Samson to continue their trek in the creek. This seemed to be the best way for now; hopefully no one following would be the wiser. However, Cutler was said to be a good tracker and if he was involved… Hannah shook her head; not wanting to think about the consequences of this.

A quick unexpected movement in the bushes at her left indicated she was no longer alone. Halting her movement forward, Hannah leaned over to reach for the rifle she'd replaced in the boot.

"No need for that," a quiet deep voice stated. "I mean you no harm."

Hannah looked up to see a tall, broad shouldered man that would easily overshadow Hiram and all his cronies, standing on the bank. His hair gleamed black as a raven's wing and the darkness of his complexion indicated he was a man who spent a lot of time in the outdoors. He didn't appear threatening and strangely enough she felt no unease. Looking up into a pair of bemused black eyes, she blushed furiously.

"What do you want? I mean… What are you doing here?"

"I was actually chasing my supper till you came along. I guess now I'll have to settle for something smaller," he replied. "What are you doing here?"

His question brought Hannah quickly to her senses and she realized time was passing.

"I have to be going. Hope you find your supper."

Giving Samson's side a quick nudge, they splashed quickly down the stream leaving the tall stranger behind. Strange that she wasn't shook up from fear, but this unfamiliar awareness of a man as handsome instead of threatening was a new sensation.

"No time for this girl," she laughed, "best get these thoughts out of your mind."

After what seemed like miles, the old Hinton place came in sight and she rode up the creek bank, pausing to fill the empty canteen she had forgotten about earlier and look the homestead over. Aware that it could be occupied by more than four legged furry creatures, she angled Samson behind a stand of cane to watch the house for any movement. It would be just her luck that one of Hiram's buddies would be of holed up in there. It would be a good place to bed down in for the night. The walls still stood erect, the roof intact, it would provide good shelter, but, it was too close to Hiram's.

Moving slowly, Hannah guided Samson along the edge of the forest, making it possible to dart behind the trees should she spot someone. At last, satisfied no one was around, Hannah rode on, still keeping as far from the house as possible in case she'd missed something. As the girl and her horse rode deeper into the woods, she mused frantically about her destination Wandering this forest for any length of time would surely get her caught – if only she knew the names of other towns. Expelling a calming breath, she began to recall numerous escape plans that the gang discussed – various towns and the ones they favored.

Immediately, the little town of Jasmine in the Northeast corner of the state came to mind. She'd heard Hiram say it bordered Memphis, Tennessee and if she could get to Memphis... the plan suddenly became clear. From there she'd cross the river, head west, and keep moving, which is what it would take to evade Hiram and Cutler. They would be relentless in their pursuit, especially once they discovered she had the LeClair jewels.

Cutler was another reason for going to Jasmine. He'd raged vehemently about the number of Yankee soldiers the gang had run into there last month. Apparently, he was obsessed with avoiding the boys in blue; riding miles around a town if they were occupying it. No one in the gang appeared to know why nor she had ever heard anyone question him about it. They just complied with his demands.

"Yep," Hannah nodded, heading north was the safest way to go.

She wouldn't be able to take Samson that far. The horse was simply too noticeable, she couldn't chance it. Hiram would be angry about her getting away, but he'd reach boiling point over his horse being gone. There would be notices posted everywhere offering lots of money to the first person who found and returned his horse.

There had been numerous offers for Samson's purchase over the years. The animal's stamina and surefooted speed was almost legend among the riffraff of Trader's Bluff; to say the horse was valuable was an understatement. On second thought, perhaps she would take Samson with her, at least to Memphis. Once there, she could sell him.

Hannah was suddenly struck by an idea that made her laugh out loud, "I'll find a Yankee officer for Samson! Wouldn't Hiram choke on that?"

Her amusement was interrupted by a loud rumbling overhead, signaling the arrival of one of the South's common spring occurrences, a thunderstorm. A strong, cool wind set the trees in motion, their newly formed leaves thrashing about wildly. Hannah stopped to watch the rolling clouds as their billowing masses changed from gray to deep purple before turning black. Not wanting to be caught in the open, she decided to look for shelter.

She spotted a trail of sorts heading uphill and decided to veer off course, hoping to find a rock house or an overhang to huddle under. Urging Samson through a maze of rhododendrons and honeysuckle, they found exactly what she was looking for. It looked like a cave with an opening somewhat obscured by various brambles and dangling vines. Provided it was deep enough and unoccupied, it should work. How many times had she searched out such shelters to stay in hiding from Hiram?

Hannah dismounted to peer inside the opening, while keeping a firm grip on the reins. It looked empty, but all the same she picked up a hefty stone and tossed it inside. It might be void of humans, but animals startled awake or protecting their young could be just as dangerous. Thankfully, all she managed to stir up was a deep thunk as the rock bounced off the back wall to roll harmlessly inside the cavern.

The structure turned out to be a rectangular room roughly 5x9 feet deep, with its left back wall rising to around seven feet before gradually arcing down to the opposite side. It would definitely provide a safe haven for the night; at least they wouldn't get soaked. Thick honeysuckle hanging over the opening would catch most of the rain, unless the wind became too fierce.

Leading the horse inside posed no problems, apparently Samson was as eager to get out of the rain as she was. However, aware that he might bolt for home after the storm, Hannah tethered him to a large boulder as far back from the opening as possible. Working quickly, she took care of his needs first; checking hooves, rubbing him down, and of course, the usual water and feed. According to Hiram, a horse's needs were more important than his rider's, especially if escape depended on that animal.

Once finished, she returned to the front to watch the storm. The lowering skies still provided enough light to see that her vantage point afforded a good view of the trail leading up to the shelter. So, with careful surveillance, she could use the rifle and easily pick-off any of Hiram's men if they made it this far. It would be that or go back to the cabin, but that wasn't going to happen.

She'd been a prisoner there for the past five years; alone and scared since her mother died. Irene LeClair Todd Walters had survived a little less than a year after losing her beloved home in Oxford and coming to "Hiram's wretched little hovel", another name she applied to the cabin. It was never referred to as "*home*".

The reality of living in such squalor along with the brutal treatment her husband now had no fears of inflicting, instilled a self-pitying bitterness that became a destructive force, and she rapidly succumbed to a consuming malaise that sapped her will to live until death was inevitable. Hannah was only 13 years old when this occurred.

Following Irene's death, Hiram pawned Hannah off on Queenie, a disgusting woman that owned the boarding house in Traders Bluff. Her instructions were to make sure Hannah learned to cook and clean. She ran away once, only to be caught and brought back. As reprimand, Queenie had beaten her with a cane pole; the first of many such punishments to follow.

Finally, after a year of this, Hannah convinced Hiram the lessons were complete and promised not to run away if he'd let her stay at the cabin whenever the gang had to be away. Hiram relented only after he and Cutler described in detail what would happen if she broke her promise. Grimacing disdainfully, she recalled how often she'd wished to be back at Queenie's.

Hannah shook her head as memories came flooding back; that life on eggshells existence when the gang needed to hole up and the immense relief that occurred every time they rode away. She made good use of their trips away. Using her papa's pistol, she'd practice shooting and became proficient at hitting targets. She also practiced with Hiram's spare rifle and was soon bringing down deer and other wild animals to supplement the meager foodstuffs Hiram provided.

No one bothered to question how she'd gained such abilities. They were too busy filling their bellies with fresh meat. Far be it for one of them to go hunting, but they'd sure made short work of her efforts; however, the rifle and ammunition were always put back in place once hunting was over. It wouldn't do for her to have access to weapons; she might shoot one of them.

Actually, thoughts of shooting Hiram or any of the gang didn't come to mind for a long time. Oh, she'd often hoped they would leave and never come back; figuring they'd be killed in one of their lawless activities. But doing it herself was unthinkable or at least it had been until last year. Since then, many of her nights were filled with dreams about knocking off her stepfather and Cutler.

Hannah shook her head in derision. Most girls her age dreamed of parties, pretty dresses, and beaus; not her, she had dreams of killing men. Well, it didn't say much for her character, but from here on out she'd better be prepared to shoot anyone that threatened harm.

A bright streak of lightning ripped across the clouds as thunder rolled, shaking the earth with its force. Moments later, a torrential rain began, jarring Hannah from her contemplations on killing. She glanced up, watching the rain fall in sheets. Surely the gang wouldn't head out in this, but she found herself praying quietly.

"Please God, let it last all night. Please? I know it's been a long time since I bothered you… I-I hope you haven't forgot me."

This had been her fearful notion for quite a while now. She sighed tiredly, remembering why such a thought had arisen.

She'd learned about Jesus as a child; how he loved and took care of everyone. This belief was a comfort, even when her papa went to war. But after he was killed in battle and her mother married Hiram, she began to have doubts, especially when everyone kept avoiding her childish questions of why. Unfortunately, life over the next five years went from bad to worse, especially after her mother died and the only parental figure available for her was Hiram Walters. He'd made fun of her nightly ritual of kneeling to pray, so that soon went by the wayside as did praying in bed since she always went to sleep before finishing.

As she developed from a skinny kid with freckles and pigtails to a young girl, life got even tougher. Suddenly, the inconvenient brat was gone and was replaced by a taller, curvier, and pretty temptation. Her burgeoning breasts were the worst part, she frowned looking down at her now flattened chest. Her mother once said these were a woman's greatest natural assets. Hannah snorted disgustedly. They'd been a detriment to her ever since they popped out.

The gang would watch her like salivating dogs as she cooked and tidied the cabin. Nights were even worse, when they drank and drooled like idiots while cheating each other at poker. Here, they'd make up some excuse for her to come to the table and reach out to grab her or pull her on their lap, making lewd remarks about what they could do. The rest would sit there hooting and egging their lucky crony on all the while chiming in, "*I'm next, I'm next!*"

She shuddered remembering the feel of their dirty hands. This, coupled with their fascination for her *'fiery red hair'* was enough to force Hannah to take drastic measures. She chopped off the curly copper tresses short enough to keep hidden beneath a hat or bandanna, and once her chest became too noticeable, she wrapped it with a wide swath of cloth that obscured any further growth. Unfortunately, her actions didn't repel the men's lewd advances, especially Hiram's. He'd demanded a so called a *'special'* payment from her.

She'd just turned fourteen the first time he tried to bed her. Catching her asleep, he was almost on her before she awoke and fought furiously until he'd given up with promises for revenge. She'd slept in the woods up a tree, that night.

The next night he tried again, but this time she was ready. Just as he pulled back the covers, she cracked him in the head with an iron skillet, sending him sprawling to a chair.

She'd then promised to poison his food, his whiskey, or anything else he swallowed if he ever tried it again. Following that, he'd stayed away from the bed but found other ways to torture her.

Hannah often thought about leaving, but there was no one to go to and nowhere else to go. However, by her 16th birthday, she'd decided any place would be better and slipped away. The results of this instilled a fear that kept her captive until today. Cutler had been sent to retrieve her.

This man was known for his ruthless actions, and that day, Hannah learned his brutality was far worse than Hiram's beatings. He'd found her, thrown her to the ground and forcibly ruined her, then lassoed her like a horse, driving her to either run all the way back to the cabin or be dragged there. The rest of that night was a well-remembered lesson in pain and humiliation. Even now, she could still see his cold soulless eyes staring her down.

"*No,*" Hannah flinched pushing, away thoughts of Cutler. She just figured God had forgotten about her. Suddenly, the forest crackled with a sizzling loud pop as lightning struck a tall dead tree, causing her to jump. The storm was fierce now and again Hannah heard herself praying for safety and an all-nighter to wash away any tracks the gang could follow. This was the most she'd prayed since her mother died. Hannah couldn't believe her temerity, picturing God up there wondering who was talking to him.

She shivered and longed for the comfort of a fire but knew a flickering light this high up would be noticeable and she couldn't take the chance of drawing anyone's attention. Watching the rain lash the trees, an image of the man she had met earlier today flashed across her mind. She wondered who he was and for some reason hoped he wasn't another vagrant or outlaw.

"Girl, you best put these thoughts away!"

Her stomach grumbled noisily, a reminder there hadn't been time to eat today, so digging out the biscuits and rabbit, she settled back to munch and watch the wind's ferocity as hail began to fall, bouncing off the surrounding rocks and foliage.

Her thoughts returned to the mess she'd left Hiram in. Had he regained consciousness or was he still lying motionless in the floor, bleeding. This image confirmed that she hadn't outright killed him. After all, dead people don't bleed, and that wound was sure enough bleeding. Hannah felt a brief sense of relief; at least they'd have no reason to put a rope around her neck; provided he didn't bleed to death.

Swallowing the last bite of her cold supper, Hannah reached for the bedroll and wrapped up. The storm had ushered in some cold air. Refusing to think any further, she yawned widely and curled on her side to keep from leaning against her sore back.

Tugging hard to pull her shirt down, she felt a sticky sensation as it resisted shifting with the rest of her clothing. No doubt some of the lash wounds had broken open and were draining. Wincing painfully, she reached out to pull the rifle closer. Yup, they'd need to be cleaned tomorrow; too bad there wasn't any whiskey around. It might sting like the devil, but it did a good job of keeping her sores cleaned out.

Hannah laid her head on the carpetbag and listened to the wind.

"Please God," she began to pray earnestly, "I know you're up there. Before today, I haven't prayed since I was a kid, so if you forgot about me, well, I suppose I deserve that. I-I'm sorry, LORD… I I. I don't even know if I'm praying right, but my nanny used to say all we have to do is ask sincerely. Dear LORD, I didn't intend to kill Hiram, I just wanted to keep him from hitting me again. I don't want to hurt anyone… I-I'm not like that bunch back there… but I can't go back and live like that… please help. Don't let them find me," she whispered before surrendering to the sleep her exhausted body could no longer hold off.

Chapter Two

Four horses sloshed steadfastly across the muddy field, heading toward a beaten path that wound through a dense forest and up an immense bluff to Hiram's hideout. Their riders seemed undisturbed by the steady downpour that was rapidly soaking anything that wasn't covered.

"Pshew wee Pinky, I can still smell that little gal's perfume on you. What'd she do? Give you a bath in it," Elam snickered, slowing his mount to drop back alongside of the young boy riding in the rear.

"Hey Elam, why didn't you grab some of that little gal," Ellis hollered from his position up front.

"Never saw a woman that looks so much like a horse in all my born days, long face, long teeth, yep, that was one for the pasture! Had you going though, didn't she boy? Yes sir, ready to fix you up good," he cackled leeringly.

Pinky dropped his head seemingly to wipe rain from his face, hoping it would help cover his embarrassment. He'd never felt comfortable in saloons and was usually ordered to stay outside and keep watch, but for some reason, Hiram had insisted he come in today. Initially, Pinky thought the boss may have actually cared that he would be soaked to the skin standing outside, but no.

He soon found out he was the subject for sport as the saloon girl made a great show of rubbing her body all over him, sitting on his lap, and pulling his face in a place where it hadn't been since he was a baby. Pinky shook his head recalling how smothering it had been between the woman's perfume, her body odor, and those melon sized bosoms.

"Aw, shut up Ellis, you're just jealous 'cause she wouldn't rub on you! It's a shame you smelled so bad no one would have you… not for any price," Elam good-naturedly teased his twin.

"Aw, come on, Rosie pleeeese," he mocked his brother's earlier efforts, "I give you $10."

Elam winked at Pinky before continuing in exaggerated outrage, "$10," he paused for effect, "whoever heard of paying any woman even $5 for a kiss? That's sure some high price spoonin'! Ain't never seen a woman worth that much," he shook his head laughing while maneuvering his horse around a large puddle that had formed in the trail.

The rain was quickly turning their track into a quagmire of deep waterholes and sticky mud that sucked at the horses' hoofs, making travel arduous.

"All of you shut up," Cutler, their sullen leader hollered back, bringing his horse to a halt.

He dismounted, squatting down to examine the animal's leg, running his hands cautiously up-and-down the flinching limb while muttering in a low tone. All joking subsided as they stopped, but hung back a little, waiting for the expected vitriolic eruption that would occur if something was wrong with his mount.

"Son of a..." the tirade began, causing the horse to draw back from the loud anger in his rider's voice. It probably would've bolted if said rider hadn't held the reins so tightly.

Everyone sat quietly, not wanting to further incite the volatile situation. They knew Cutler's temper, knew he'd just as soon shoot someone as to look at him or her or it, whichever was providing the source of irritation. Hiram may have fancied himself the leader of the gang, but he lacked this man's enjoyment and willingness to implement authority. Where Hiram was more amicable and persuasive, Cutler was the vilest and most dangerous; quick to shoot to kill with no questions asked.

The incensed man rose from examining the horse; his tall, rail thin stature topped by a face exuding resentment and cruelty. A hook nose and close-set eyes served to give him the appearance of a ravenous hawk always in search of his next prey. A scar that curved down from his left eye to just under his chin tended to heighten this appearance.

He cursed vehemently as the skies opened and what had been a steady shower turned into a torrential onslaught of hail.

"Get off your horse," he yelled at Pinky, "and don't give me no whinin' lip."

"But… but what am I gonna do?" Pinky asked in direct disregard of the warning.

Elam and Ellis shook their heads, wondering at either Pinky's temerity or his lack of common sense. No one questioned the Brit, especially in this state of temper. Not bothering to answer, Cutler spun around, stalked to Pinky's horse, and jerked him out of the saddle, flinging him to the soggy ground.

"Walk, crawl, or slither on your belly; don't matter to me, but your horse is mine now or at least until my horse's leg heals." Having said this, he climbed into the saddle and rode away, leading the injured horse.

Lightning split the sky and the partners kind of straggled along, choosing not to follow too closely to their seething leader. Pinky picked himself up and began the long muddy walk, hunching his shoulders against the hail. The mud pulled at his boots making walking awkward and after several stumbles and another sprawl face down on the wet ground, Elam finally took pity on him.

"Here," he called riding back and kicking his foot free of the stirrup, "Mount up; we'll never get there with you lolly-gaggin' behind.

Reckon my horse can carry us both. Just don't lean too close and rub any of that perfume on me," he snickered.

"Much obliged Elam," Pinky mumbled settling in to ride double.

The group continued their waterlogged journey, a much quieter less jovial bunch as they entered the forest, winding their way through a thick growth of trees towards Hiram's. The cabin sat at the top of a high bluff, providing an excellent lookout for strangers or any lawmen that might come nosing around. Occasionally, an old peddler stopped by, but he was as much a thief as anyone in the gang, therefore posing no threat.

The cabin was the result of a poker game with an old sea captain in New Orleans. Hiram had trounced him; filling his pockets with $500 cash, a gold pocket watch, and the deed to a dwelling in some place called Trader's Bluff, Mississippi. He didn't pay much attention to it, having no intention of ever leaving his hometown. However, circumstances changed and once you started running from the law you certainly had to have somewhere to hole up in. The isolation of the cabin was ideal.

It wasn't much to look at. Time and the elements had definitely battered the once sturdy structure. It now sat kind of crooked, with one corner dropping below the rest as if the ground under that corner was sinking away. It presented a gray, drab weathered appearance with cracks between the logs where chinking had fallen out over the years. A small lone window afforded its occupants a modicum of light, but that too appeared gray with its dirty coating.

Hiram wanted it left that way, insisting light couldn't reflect off dirt and draw attention to their location. He had done little work to the place; not even when he brought Irene and Hannah to live there. The inside wasn't any better than the outside, providing a main room with a fireplace that served as a gathering place, cooking space, and sleeping quarters all in one. A small room to the side was reserved for Hiram and his *woman*.

He did concede to make one upgrade. He and the twins built a barn that included bunks for the gang, stalls for the horses, and a tack room. The latter also served as storage for any loot that didn't get sold or bartered after their raids. Any other improvements to the place would occur only if absolutely necessary.

Hiram figured his talents were best suited to ordering others around, outsmarting the law, and charming women, mostly the working girls in Traders Bluff's taverns. He often bragged about his prowess for beguiling women. His favorite boast was his conquest of the rich widow Todd, pretending to be a fine Southern gentleman, concerned about the welfare of that genteel beauty. He'd rub his hands together in glee and guffaw over how easy it had been to woo the lady.

"Like squeezing milk from an old cow's udder, a little squeeze here, a little squeeze there," he'd smack his lips and leer suggestively at his wife, when she was alive, and then later at Hannah.

Unfortunately for Irene and Hannah, Hiram was a lazy, shiftless no account whose goal in life was to use a woman for what he could get off her; money, property, bed partner… He'd take it all until finally she was dead; which is just what he did to Irene. When they married, she'd been a wealthy society belle with plenty of Yankee dollars in the bank and the owner of a vast plantation. She died a penniless, broken, social nobody; finally escaping her plight in death. She was now buried somewhere out back of the cabin without a marker to show she ever existed.

Thunder rumbled ominously and the wind picked up as the silent group trudged slowly on; each one ruefully contemplating their miserable state.

Elam ventured to comment, "Hope Hannah's made some biscuits and gravy. I'm so hungry my belly's layin' over my backbone. I don't think I've et since yesterdiy mornin'."

"Yeah," Ellis agreed, "she's a right good cook."

"Pretty too," Pinky remarked.

"Yeah," Ellis agreed, "she's sure filled out. I thought that girl was nothin' but a beanpole with short red hair till I come on her bathin' at the stream one day. Boy, you ought to see her!"

"If you got any brains," Cutler growled, "you'll keep them kind of thoughts inside that head of yours or Hiram'll be pluggin' you to the wall. Hannah's his property; she done took her mother's place."

Cutler wheeled his horse around, "if you fellas know what's good for you, you'll keep your mouth shut and you better not let me, or Hiram, catch you followin' Hannah to the stream again."

He ended this brief rebuke by giving Pinky a withering cold glare that dared further comment. Finally, he turned his horse around and galloped ahead. Everyone came to an immediate halt as Cutler pulled up short and held up his hand for silence. The cabin was in plain view and each man puzzled over why they were stopping in this storm when shelter was just a few yards ahead.

Ellis caught up quickly, "Why're you stopped?" he asked quietly.

Cutler snorted impatiently, his eyes darting quickly from one run down object to the other.

"Look yonder;" he nodded his head toward the house, "somethin' here's not right."

The four men warily scrutinized the scene before them. No one said a word as they studied the old cabin and barn.

"See," he pointed, "no lantern burnin', no wood smoke from the chimney, clothes still hangin', even in the rain… somethin's wrong," he said getting off Pinky's horse and taking out his revolver.

"Yeah," Ellis agreed, following his lead.

Dismounting, he instructed Pinky and Elam, "Stay put in case we have to ride out fast."

Elam and Pinky watched as their partners dodged quickly from tree to rock to bush in case someone was watching from the inside. After several intense minutes, Cutler aimed his gun in the air, firing off three shots in rapid succession. Pistols drawn… they all hesitated, waiting for return gunfire; however, the steady drum of rain was the only audible sound.

Cutler motioned Ellis, and together they cautiously approached the front of the cabin until each man was flanking the front door on either side.

Ellis silently mouthed, "one… two… three," and they stormed through the door, guns firing.

Stopping suddenly, they were shocked by the sight they'd almost stumbled over. There, in the middle of the floor, now bloody from a weeping gash on the back of his head lay Hiram moaning and trying to get up.

"What happened here?" Cutler demanded, squatting down beside the wounded man.

Hiram finally managed to roll over and with his partners help rise to a sitting position. Ellis noticed another bloody gash running from Hiram's ear to his chin and pointed silently to it.

Exchanging a puzzled look with Cutler, he asked, "Hiram cain"t ya hear us? What the Sam hill went on here… 'cause it's plain that some kind of ruckus come off and from the look of it you didn't come out so good?"

Hiram groaned, shaking his head, but stopped immediately since the action only increased the harsh pain that seemed to reverberate from one side of his skull to the other.

"I… I can't recall right now," he managed to mumble.

He sat there befuddled, looking between his two buddies as if they could provide some answers. Reaching a shaking hand up to his face, he meant to wipe his chin, but was stopped by Cutler.

"Leave it be, I need to wipe it off and see how bad that cut is; Hannah may have to sew it up."

"Yeah," Ellis echoed looking around the cabin, "unless she's tied up somewhere, or whoever did this, took her with 'em."

Elam ventured in cautiously, weapon readied for action only to re-holster it upon spying a muddled Hiram in the floor.

Pinky stumbled in last to mutter before thinking, "man, what happened here?"

No one said a word as Hiram sat wavering unsteadily back and forth, holding his head in his hands.

Pinky suddenly burst out, "looks like Hiram tangled with a bear."

He caught the words abruptly, while silently calling himself ten kind of a fool. Would he ever learn to keep his mouth shut? Standing stiffly, he watched retribution approach. Cutler strode silently up to the boy pausing to stand nose to nose. Several pounding heartbeats later, he began walking slowly pushing the young man until his back was against the door.

"Shut up and get that whiskey out of my saddlebag and pitch it here," he ordered, "Then take the horses to the barn and give 'em food and water and rub 'em down too."

Pinky flushed a shade of red that endorsed the nickname Cutler had given him, silently hating the cowardly feeling of impotence the outlaw's threats instilled. Had he always been this chicken hearted... well, he was tired of cowering!

"Hey now, I ain't no slave," he countered. "I think ever'one ought to take care of his own horse."

His breath ceased as the muzzle of a pistol prodded his belly followed by an ominous click.

"Now," Cutler snarled, "You'll be anything we tell you to be or you won't be at all," he paused to let the implication of his words sink in, "is that clear?"

The room was deathly silent as everyone waited for a complicit response. At last, a subdued Pinky nodded and slowly edged sideways to comply. Elam and Ellis exchanged a silent look, each wondering how long it would be before Cutler killed the kid. Cause if the young boy didn't learn to keep his mouth shut and take orders, the Brit was sure to either plug him dead or beat him to death.

Elam caught the bottle of whiskey Pinky tossed in, handed it over, then headed out to help with the horses. Cutler squatted wordlessly while opening the bottle and placed it securely in Hiram's shaking hands.

"Here, drink this," he demanded, "maybe it'll clear your head a bit and you can tell us what went on here."

Ellis agreed and hunkered down on the other side of Hiram, waiting anxiously as he took several long swigs from the bottle. The old clock on the shelf ticked noisily amplifying the tension in the room. Cutler sprang up and began prowling restlessly, looking in every corner checking Hiram's room and behind the curtain were Hannah slept.

Frustration echoed in every audible breath he exhaled and whirling around he yelled, "Hiram," causing all of them to jump.

"What went on here today? Were you robbed? Did Sam Parton's bunch catch up with us? Did they find that last stash we took off of 'em?" He waited again, "Well man," he roared.

Hiram continued to waiver unsteadily; silently nursing the whiskey bottle.

Watching Hiram intensely Cutler directed, "Ellis, get a rag and water and wipe up them wounds. From the looks of things Hannah's not here, so I guess I'll be doin' the sewin' and I cain't sew it if I cain't see it."

Elam reentered the cabin only to be told to check out back for any signs of struggle.

"What are you lookin' out there for? You know there'll be no tracks, the rain done washed 'em away."

Cutler shook his head and waved his arm toward the door.

"Well," he yelled impatiently, "look in the barn see if anything's missin' there."

Ellis caught his twin's eye and motioned him toward the door; no need to raise Cutler's temper any higher.

"Best to do as you're told," he mouthed.

Elam went back out in the storm and Ellis began tending Hiram's head.

"It's a wonder you ain't dead," he mumbled quietly. "These are some bad gashes. What'd they use on you anyway?"

Hiram remained silent, flinching as the rag passed over the injured areas.

"Looks like it's gonna take a lot of stitches," Ellis remarked.

"I said I'd do it," Cutler growled, "if we don't find Hannah. I've sewed up worse 'n that. We'll just have to get him good and liquored up."

He continued roaming around the room, his sharp eye taking in every corner and open space searching for some clue that might shed light on what had taken place.

Approaching the fireplace, he picked up the poker lying half in half out of the dead ashes and with close inspection spied the dried blood covering its end.

"This is what they used on you," he announced shoving the sharp pointed iron rod in Hiram's face, "see, see the blood."

Hiram shrank back from the offending weapon trying his best to pull his scattered thoughts together. He took another fast swig from the bottle, wincing painfully as he tilted his head to swallow. The alcohol was having a pretty rapid effect and as Hiram examined his arms and hands and finally his legs.

He laughed drunkenly and quipped, "Look boys my foot's layin' backwards."

At this, Cutler exploded, viciously kicking the artificial leg. "Who cares about that bloody leg," he yelled. "Cain't you remember nothin'?" He stomped away angrily.

"By the way, where"s Hannah... did something happen to her, or..." he suddenly broke off having glimpsed Hiram's bullwhip.

It must have been caught underneath him when he fell. Cutler eyed the whip, then Hiram, then the poker and a mental picture began taking shape in his mind. He squatted down face-to-face with the injured man asking quietly, "Did Hannah do this to you?"

The cabin door burst open, allowing Elam and Pinky to stumble in the room. Pausing to wipe the rain out of his eyes, Elam held up a wooden box inscribed with the words Monsieur Flaubert's Salon, Paris, France.

"Look what we found in the barn," he announced.

"Whereabouts in the barn," Cutler asked, staring intently at the box.

"Looks like it was dug up from that back corner stall where we pile leftover goods; 'ppears it was buried under the straw and dirt. There's a good-sized hole left," Elam continued.

Cutler stomped over and grabbed the box, examining it closely.

"Didn't Irene keep her jewelry in a box like this?" he demanded, pushing the cedar container in Hiram's hands.

Hiram shook his head, a vibrating anger overriding any thoughts of pain this motion caused as he examined the empty wooden chest.

"I knew she had 'em," he raged throwing the box across the room. "I looked and looked for them stones. She told me them house slaves took 'em when they left Oxford. Should've known better… Should've… Just think, all this time…"

He didn't finish the thought, instead taking another drink he answered Cutler's earlier question, "Yeah, it's all coming back… that ungrateful little heifer, Hannah, did this to me. Remember it now… She tried to kill me. Where is she? I'm gonna teach her a lesson she won't ever forget… Just wait till…"

Cutler interrupted Hiram's outburst, "We cain't find Hannah, she ain't nowhere around."

"Oh, she's around," he argued assuredly. "She's hidin' out in the woods till we all leave. She ain't gone far."

Elam cleared his throat quietly before telling the next bit of explosive information, "Um, Hiram," he began slowly, "I'm afraid somethin' else is missin'…" He shuffled from one to foot to the other nervously.

"Well man, spit it out," Hiram demanded.

"Samson's gone." Elam related this while backing up beside Pinky, who was hovering around the door, ready to dash out when the expected explosion ensued.

It didn't take long, as Cutler and Hiram let loose a list of vitriolic expletives that described no mercy for Hannah, when they found her, and sure retribution for anyone that stepped in their way.

Pinky for once sensed the situation and exited the front door, circling around to enter the back of the cabin. Given Cutler and Hiram's moods, he wasn't fool enough to walk in front of them. They'd probably use him as a stand-in for Hannah and after hearing their plans for her… well, the less noticeable he made himself, the better off he'd be. He decided to make supper and upon examining the shelves discovered Hannah had also cleaned them out of canned goods. Capturing

Elam's attention, he discreetly motioned him over and pointed this out.

"At least she left the coffee an' flour an' stuff," Elam grumbled under his breath.

He too had no wish to draw anyone's attention, it would be like pourin' whiskey on an already blazing fire. The two men set about making coffee and some semblance of supper.

Things quieted down as Cutler, with Ellis assisting, concentrated on sewing up Hiram's wounds. The exception to this was a frequent curse from the now inebriated patient, who in one breath reviled Hannah and next his dead wife. The unpleasant ordeal seemed to drag by, but finally with one last stitch, the injuries were closed, and Hiram slumped over in a drunken stupor, still mumbling about "women an' jewelry an' whores… all of em!" He roared before giving in to unconsciousness. Cutler and Ellis grudgingly packed him into the side room and dumped him on the bed.

Returning to the room, Ellis busied himself with starting a fire as Cutler walked over to glare out the dirt encrusted window at the offending storm. It was not only wiping away any possibility for tracking but was also keeping him cooped up here. He stood there slamming one fist into the palm of his other hand… feeling the need for action like slamming someone's brains out. It made no difference about the type of action as long as it afforded a release for the frenzied agitation that came over him when he felt someone else had won a score that should've been his. He turned and paced back to the fire, squatting down to stare intently into its flames.

Pinky started to say something, but Ellis caught him, shaking his head negatively, quietly imploring the boy to keep his mouth shut. Elam silently let the others know the food was ready. They all grabbed a plate except Cutler, who waited about halfway through their meal before demanding sarcastically, "A cup of that coffee might be good."

Ellis complied without comment as Cutler continued undaunted… issuing orders with that same commanding manner.

"In the morning, Elam, you an' Pinky go into Traders Bluff and ask around if anyone's seen a tall, red haired girl come to town. Tell em you're expectin' Hiram's niece and if they see anyone like that… tell em to take her to Queenie over at the Boardin' House. You're to say she's a new whore, come to sell her wares and they're not to let anybody have her till I get there. Queenie will know better than to cross me!"

"Are you sure you want Elam and Pinky to take care of that?" Ellis questioned hesitantly. "You know that boy has a habit of runnin' his mouth when he ought not."

Cutler glared at Pinky until he was ready to run from the room and finally stated, "if you mess this up boy, Elam may as well kill you there, cause," he paused to then glare at Elam, "if I hear these instructions get messed up by any word, when you get back, I'm not only gonna kill the boy... I'm gonna kill Ellis. So, you better control him, Elam, even if you have to gag him."

"Why not just leave him here," Elam ventured.

"Cause I'm staying here in case Hannah comes slinking back and I don't want him around," Cutler growled turning back to the fire.

Ellis poured more coffee and asked no one in particular, "What are we gonna do about Samson?"

Cutler answered thoughtfully. "If Hannah doesn't come back by tomorrow night, I'll go to town an' see if anybody's turned up. I'll put out the word that Hiram's horse was stolen too and offer a reward for the person that finds it. Guess I better pick up a couple more horses for Hiram and me too... cause boys if that wench doesn't show up here like Hiram says she will... we're sure goin' after her."

Fretting over the threat to kill his brother, Elam assured him that orders would be followed and quickly changed the subject hoping to get Cutler's mind off killing, "How much y'all think that jewelry was worth?" he asked quietly.

"Don't know for sure," Ellis replied, "but I heard Hiram say some of them jewels came from French kings and queens; said all of it together was probably worth around $10, 000."

"$10, 000," Pinky echoed incredulously. "I ain't ever seen anything..." he broke off abruptly as Cutler stood to send him a menacing glare.

For a moment, the air seemed to quiver with his suppressed anger, and everyone appeared frozen… waiting for something to break or explode… anything to relieve the desperate tension that held them all in its grip. Finally, the enraged outlaw stomped across the room to storm out the cabin door. Watching its loose boards stop quivering, Pinky let out a breath of heartfelt relief that he had again escaped the bloody Brit's *retribution.*

Making his way over to Hannah's curtained off corner, he sank wearily down on the bed realizing this was the third time today he'd set off Cutler's temper.

"Way to go idiot! Shoot your mouth off one more time and he'll sure enough end your sorry life."

Shaking his head miserably, the boy wondered how he was ever going to escape this gang. Never had he imagined to be a part of something like this; for while he didn't have any kinfolk now, he'd had a ma and pa for his first 15 years and they'd brought him up to know stealing, whoring, and killing people wasn't the right way to live. Thinking about his family brought a wealth of unshed tears and he laid back, placing an arm across his eyes so the shirt sleeve would soak up any telling moisture. At least they'd never know what his life had become.

He'd been born Calvin Simmons only son of George and Lucille Simmons in Helena, Arkansas. His parents ran the county land agents' office and lived in the provided housing that encompassed the entire top floor of the building. It wasn't overly large or anything fancy, but it satisfied the needs of their three-membered family, or it had until Sam Whitaker, insisting he'd been cheated out of his land, set fire to the building, resulting in its total loss along with the lives of George and Lucille. Pinky had been away from home that night and carried a sense of guilt ever since; believing that if he'd been there, he could've saved them.

His guilt had driven him away from Helena and he ended up in Fayetteville, working various odd jobs; earning enough to pay for a room and his food. He built up a reliable reputation and was regarded by the townsfolk as a nice young man, ready to help out anyone that asked. A couple of months after his 17th birthday, he'd decided to head to Fort Smith and join the military.

But the day he was ready to leave circumstances intervened. He'd just rode up to the town's new bank and dismounted when four men came running out the front door; their guns blazing and faces covered. One of them thrust a bag of money into his hands and at gunpoint ordered him to mount up and ride. Pinky paused long enough for the outlaw to shoot a hole through the sleeve of his shirt.

"Boy," the outlaw growled, "ride or die. It's your choice."

That was seven months ago. Pinky shuddered, so far all they'd made him do was hold the horses during the last two raids, but the people they'd shot, and Cutler's treatment of the women gave him a sick stomach every time he relived it. He couldn't go through that again. There had to be away out of this mess.

Pinky lay quietly desperately trying to devise a plan for escape. Elam and Ellis weren't so bad, just two misguided souls with misplaced loyalties. However, Hiram and Cutler were the kind of men one knew better than to cross. Cutler had repeatedly promised to kill him if he tried to leave; swearing the gang would hunt him down.

Pinky shuddered, remembering the outlaw's mocking sneer as he declared, "*You see boy, you belong to me now... body and soul. I can do anything to you, and nobody will stop me... see,*" he'd emphasized this by placing his pistol at Pinky's temple and clicking on an empty chamber. And while the boy had almost passed out, the man he'd come to regard as evil incarnate had laughed maniacally and waved his hand to include the rest of the gang, "*See, not one of these men will step up to save ya... you're mine!*"

Pinky had never considered himself a coward, but these men made him want to find a hole and crawl in. He shook his head in disgust at this revelation. He lay still, feigning sleep and listened to Elam and Ellis talk about Cutler's precarious state of mind. The front door opened, and the topic of conversation entered in a burst of wind and rain and glowering looks, like the storm outside was invading the cabin.

"Hiram still sleep," he demanded. At Elam's affirmative nod he threw out another questioning demand, "Where's the kid?"

Ellis answered this time, "Reckon he's asleep in Hannah's bed."

"Wake him up, I got something to say I want all of you to hear it at the same time," Cutler directed curtly, stopping in the middle of the room so as to command attention.

Elam roused Pinky and everyone, with the exception of Hiram, who continued to snore noisily in the other room, gathered around the fireplace waiting expectantly.

Cutler walked over and looked each man in the eye before stating, "From here on out I give the orders. Hiram has no say in what we do or don't do… is that clear?"

He watched each man closely ready for any objection that might be raised.

No one spoke or moved, and he continued, "Hiram's slippin', getting' soft. First, he lets that wife of his get away with lyin' about them jewels and today he lets Hannah nearly kill him. At this point, I don't think it would be a good idea to take him on any more raids. He ain't got it no more and he's liable to get us all either killed or caught."

Pinky's eyes bounced from Elam to Ellis as the twins exchanged looks before slowly turning to face the newly proclaimed leader.

Ellis began, "I know you're an able man Cutler and here lately you kind of took over anyway, but me and Elam owe our lives to Hiram and we'll wait and see what he says about this before makin' any decision to count him out."

"Why?" Cutler demanded furiously. "He ain't nothin' but a liability that's gonna get us all caught and hung. He can't ride far without stoppin' and going on about that leg of his. Besides, I'm tired of listenin' to his braggart mouth. None of you would have done as good as you have if it wasn't for me… my plans… my directions… my leadership," he emphasized this by jabbing his thumb at his chest each time he said the word '*my*'.

He broke off, his cold eyes boring into each man. He moved suddenly as though reaching for his gun but was brought up short by Ellis' quiet remark.

"If you want to start any shootin' about this," he stated beating Cutler to the draw, "we got two guns to your one… so have at it, if you're sure that's how you want things to be."

Cutler stared malevolently at the two men now facing him, with guns drawn. He nodded his head at Pinky and sneered, "Where's your gun boy?"

Pinky shrugged his shoulders, "You know I don't have a gun, but I agree with Elam and Ellis," he declared.

He didn't have anything to lose at this point; at least he could die with some self-respect. Cutler spun about and tore back out in the stormy night, slamming the cabin door noisily against the wall. The three stood silently watching as it swung wildly vibrating with the mad man's fury. Momentarily, Pinky walked over and closed it. Ellis wiped the rain that had blown in off his pistol before holstering it, while Elam retrieved the coffee pot. They all took vigil close to the fire, knowing that any sleep for them would only be caught in snatches. No one trusted their self- proclaimed leader wouldn't slit their throats while they slept.

Pinky sat down on a bare log close to the fire. Giving into curiosity he took a deep breath and looked from first Elam to Ellis before asking quietly, "How did you two meet Hiram?"

Ellis let out a brief chortle before launching into the tale of how one late night Hiram came upon two skinny males being harassed and beaten by a couple of dandies from the very rich Southworth family, a sample of New Orleans finest.

"You know, one of them families that have everything money, position, respect… Hiram said they'd looked down their noses and spit on him too many times to count. So, when he stumbled up on them beatin' up two skinny ragamuffins all of that burning anger that he'd been holding back for years took control and let me tell you he charged in cursin', spittin', and fists flyin'."

Here, Ellis paused shaking his head at the memory.

"He had things pretty well in hand 'til Elam grabbed one of their pistols that'd been knocked loose and shot one of them Southworth boys. He started to yell and carry-on 'I'm shot, I'm shot, you'll hang for this you dirty swamp scum!'"

Ellis stopped to look over at Elam, which caused the two of them to burst out laughing.

"What happened next?" Pinky asked.

"While them brothers limped away, Hiram hustled us off to some old livery stable that was falling apart and ordered us to stay hid 'til he came back. The next morning before sunrise, he was at that livery yankin' us awake and lookin' us over. I reckon he took pity on us because we were a sight, all muddy and dirty from the night's fight in the dirt. We never had clothes to fit us; they were either too short and tight or too big. Our clothes was always something' somebody gave to pa to keep us boys covered. So, all we each had on was a pair of overalls two sizes too big, no shirt, and dirty bare feet."

"Well, we was settin' there being sized up and Elam's belly lets out a powerful rumble and growl because we hadn't et anything for three days. At that point I started talkin' fast thanking this stranger for steppin' Hiram in; tellin' our names and how we was supposed to be looking for work in New Orleans. Then, Hiram just started shaking his head an' tellin' us we'd have to forget that 'cause if we didn't get out of town we was 'bout to get ourselves and him hanged."

Here, Elam joined the conversation telling Pinky how their Pa had sent them to the city find work and send money home, "Said at 17 we was growed up enough to do this."

Ellis cleared his throat and picked the storyline back up, "Hiram said, we could stay and take our chances if we wanted to, but he was leavin' and perhaps we wouldn't hang but we'd sure enough be locked up in prison. That Southworth family would make sure of that. Well, at that point me and Elam made the only choice that made sense we left out of there with Hiram. He had two horses so we two rode double and bareback till he came up with another mount and saddles. I reckon I'll never forget how the sun was just peekin' over that East horizon as we high-tailed it out of town, headin' for Texas. Hiram took care of everything horses, food, and the first decent clothing we'd ever had. He even taught us to shoot a gun. We've been together since, roamin' through the southwest; stealin', drinkin', gamblin' and socializin' all the tarts that'll have us."

He paused for a minute before giving a determined shake of his head to end his story with, "Hiram is our leader and me and Elam, we owe him our lives, and ain't no uppity

British cur ever gonna boot him out… no sir… not without a fight."

Sometime around daybreak, Hiram came stumbling to the fireplace, ordering Pinky to get him some coffee. Elam and Ellis jerked fully awake to hurriedly scoot a chair close to the fire for him.

"How's the head this mornin'?" Elam asked.

"Feels like a dang train ran over it," Hiram winced, careful not to raise his voice too loud, lest the noise aggravate the now bearable pain that persisted.

"I'm gonna kill that ungrateful witch the minute she comes back. Should have bashed her brains out when she was a snot nosed kid. Always lookin' down her nose at me… I'll give her somethin' to look down at, bury her out there with her mother!" He paused, looking around the room, "Where's Cutler?" he questioned looking from Elam to Ellis.

"Don't rightly know," Ellis began, "but we need to talk to you before he comes in." Ellis quickly told Hiram about Cutler's intention to take over the gang; repeating the scathing comments that had been made about Hiram's failing abilities and bragging tales.

They sat quietly waiting for Hiram to take in everything Ellis had related. After several quiet minutes, he cleared his throat and spoke.

"Okay boys, first, we have to get Hannah back, if she is for sure gone. She's carryin' around $10,000 worth of jewels that rightly belong to me and I aim to have them. I married that blasted woman and what was hers is mine. I don't like what Cutler said or the way he's goin' about this, but he's the best at trackin' people down and if anyone can find her, he can. I say we let him lead but come hell or high water I'm goin' along. Will you boys back me up?" He paused, looking from one man to the other.

Three heads nodded in unison.

"Okay, let me talk to him and till we find Hannah an' get that jewelry, we carry things out just as he says, but we kill him after this… if he don't kill us first. Keep your guard up boys."

Again, each man solemnly consented. However, Pinky knew this was it for him. He was sick of this kind of life and the first chance he got to slip away… he'd be gone.

Chapter Three

Hannah awoke to the sounds of Samson's restless movements as he whinnied and shuffled uneasily, signaling his morning routine was overdue. She sat up, wincing as sharp pains radiated from her sore back momentarily halting all movement. Immediately, the events of the day before sprang to mind and she bit down on the pain to rise hastily regardless of any discomfort the effort might cause.

It took little time to break camp. There were a few things to repack, but this was carried out along with replacing the saddle gear while the disgruntled animal chewed on his oats. Giving Samson time to finish, she moved to the front of their shelter and looked out over the freshly washed forest.

The rising sun sparkled in little crystal like raindrops that dripped from rocks, leaves, and bare branches, while a gentle breeze carried the raucous rousing of birds calling a welcome to the new day. Carefully scanning the surrounding forest, Hannah was pleased that things appeared undisturbed. Stepping out, she paused to observe the rising sun and hopefully ascertain the right direction for heading north.

"Heaven knows, it's going to be a long day in the saddle," she sighed, reentering the structure to lead Samson out. Retrieving the remains of her supper, she attempted to eat, but it was all dried out.

"Good way to break some teeth," she muttered breaking off a small bit to chew on until it was pliable enough to swallow.

It might lack flavor, but it would suffice to fill a grumbling belly for the next few hours.

The morning looked to be clear of rain, and Hannah knew that barring any mishaps or run-ins with strangers she could put a lot of miles between her and Hiram's cabin. Taking the horse's reins, she descended the hill and headed north, hopefully to Jasmine. She rode for hours, thankful for the forest canopy that provided a shield from the sun as it rose higher and became hotter. The shade of towering ash, oak, and magnolia trees was all that kept her from breaking out in a new crop of freckles. It would serve her right though… forgetting to grab a hat yesterday; wearing a hat outside was almost as natural as breathing for someone with her pale skin.

Just something else to detest about her appearance, she grimaced, reviewing her physical attributes… red hair, freckles and a big bosom. Unfortunately, the deplorable assets didn't stop there. She'd grown tall and was now taller than the men in the gang, except for Hiram. What if she towered over all other men too, unless Hiram's men were all considered runts; boy, wouldn't that just burn their pride, she grinned. Sobering quickly, Hannah accepted that she was woefully unattractive with no small and ladylike features to display.

She sometimes wondered what she looked like now, after all, the last time she'd seen a looking glass was before they left Oxford in '62. That was a little over four years ago and she'd been a tall, freckled stick with red pigtails then. She recalled her mother's uncomplimentary frowning, *'tsk, tsk, tsk'* while Nanny always said she'd be a fine beautiful lady when she grew up.

But what Hannah doubted then she was sure of now. Beautiful women didn't stand almost six feet tall and be adorned with freckles. And fine, ladies didn't go around in men's dungarees, binding their bosoms, and cutting their hair clean up to its roots. They didn't almost kill people either.

This sobering thought brought her reflections to a halt as she realized Samson was veering off course. She'd never ridden past the old Hinton Homestead and this was unfamiliar territory; getting lost here was a real possibility. There were no recognizable features to use for landmarks so if she didn't want to ramble aimlessly for days, it was best to pay attention. Sitting up straighter, Hannah once again got her bearings and hopefully set out in the right direction. Raising the canteen for a quick swallow, she realized Samson had drunk most of the water earlier. They'd need to find a stream or creek soon.

Thinking of Samson, she reached down and patted the horse's neck. He'd behaved really well so far, which according to Hiram wasn't his usual behavior when someone unfamiliar tried to ride him. The tale was that Samson would buck and throw all kinds of fits if someone other than his master sat on him. This was probably the liar's way of keeping Pinky off his horse, she smirked remembering the time Pinky tried to ride the ornery animal. Hiram blew up; nobody, not even Cutler, got on Samson.

Presently, the horse paused… his ears pricking forward as though to capture some sound. Hannah sat still, straining to see as well as listen, but picked up nothing. She took a firm hold on the reins for better control, should he decide to take off. It wouldn't take much to topple her out of the saddle. Finally, Samson settled down, but she remained watchful for any noise, sight, or feeling that could indicate danger.

About mid-day she picked up sounds of running water. Samson must have heard it too as he quickened his pace.

"Whoa boy, slow down," she urged bending painfully low to dodge a large limb.

Straightening slowly, she pulled up sharply to observe the scene before them. Sure enough, they'd found water; a wide swift stream that bubbled and plunged over rocks and small waterfalls. And while this presented a refreshing idyllic picture, its other occupants did not.

Hannah slowly backed Samson up to stand behind an enormous magnolia and reached down to pull the rifle across her lap, hoping she wouldn't have to use it, but ready just in case. They sat quietly, watching a black bear cub and its mother playing in the water. Granted it was an engaging sight, but now wasn't the time for enjoying nature's tranquil scenes, and the one ahead wouldn't be tranquil for long if that mother bear scented their presence.

Hannah reached up to wipe a trail of sweat from her eyes, fervently hoping the bears would move on without noticing them. At last, the little bear scampered out of the water and headed toward the trees in the opposite direction, causing the mother to lumber out after it.

Walking the horse slowly, she approached the water, staying seated until he had drunk his fill. Only then did she dismount, holding onto the saddle long enough to let her legs stabilize. One thing for certain, she'd have a sore backside to go along with her back tonight. Carrying the rifle and retaining the reins, Hannah filled the canteen before taking a brief rest; she daren't take long though, the Walters gang could easily be closing in.

Pushing sweaty hair off her forehead, she recalled seeing a bandanna attached to Hiram's rain slicker. Retrieving this, she spread the ragged square of cloth out for examination. It was filthy, but a few quick dips in the stream made it passable and she squeezed out the excess water before tying it around her head. At least it would keep the sweat from her eyes.

Hannah tied the horse to a small sapling and darted behind some bushes to relieve a body function that could no longer be ignored. She hurried, realizing her vulnerability if caught in this position. Returning, she slipped the rifle back in its boot and gingerly resumed the saddle, ready to set out again. But Samson had other ideas and ignored calls to move; stubbornly refusing to leave the lush grass he was cropping and in obstinate defiance lowered his backend as though to sit on his haunches. It was all Hannah could do to hang on. Gripping his sides firmly with her knees, she leaned forward over his neck to stay seated.

"You nasty beast," she scolded, "I can be just as ornery as you. So, you may as well move! Let's go!" she yelled digging her heels firmly into his side while reaching behind to deliver a stinging slap to his butt.

Giving a derisive snort, the contrary animal lunged forward just as suddenly as he had sat back and took off at a fast gallop. They flew by trees, jumped rotting logs, and dodged low hanging limbs, but somehow through sheer willpower she managed to remain in the saddle and let the critter run until he finally came to a prancing halt, blowing, and shaking his head.

Hannah sat upright slowly; her body racked with the pain of maintaining her seat throughout the horse's flight. Shaking from the fear of what had just happened and the uncertainty of what the animal might do next, she took a much-needed moment to calm down and look around to see how far off course they were. It appeared they were still headed north, so with a distrusting sense of doubt, she gave her heels a firm dig in the horse's side to urge him forward.

Thankfully, Samson seemed to have run out his contrariness and began walking in the calm manner he'd exhibited earlier. The rest of the afternoon passed without incident, but she paid closer attention to his behavior. Apparently, Hiram hadn't lied about this ornery animal after all.

They traveled until the sun lay low in the west and its last rays changed from radiant brilliance to a soft amber glow before Hannah began searching for a place to make camp. She hadn't seen any rock houses like they had stayed in the previous night, so a place off trail would have to do. Luckily, their northward path had somehow picked up the stream they'd stopped at earlier, only now it had broadened to the width of a creek with water so clear you could see fish swimming beneath the surface.

Winding their way around a house size rock, Hannah came up on a half circle of boulders that towered over seven feet high. The area within their semicircle would provide a sturdy shelter as long as it didn't rain. Thankfully it was close to the water.

Climbing slowly and wearily from the saddle, Hannah dropped to the ground with a thud as a body, unused to such long hours on a horse, crumpled in an exhausted heap. She pulled the now dry bandanna off her head, using it to wipe the sweat from her neck and face; almost too tired to move. After a while she reached up and grabbed the stirrup for leverage to help hoist her body off the ground.

"Samson, please do not move," she pleaded, rising painfully.

She ached in every part of her body, even her arms and hands, which moved sluggishly as though held down by weights. Standing stiffly, she allowed her body to adjust from its cramped position and mustering a last reserve of energy, removed the saddle, and her belongings from the horse's back, tended to his care, and made sure he was securely tethered.

It was warm enough that a fire really wasn't needed, but a small one would lend a sense of comfort and hopefully keep curious animals away. A lot of the wood lying close was still damp from yesterday's rain, but she was able to locate several dry pieces lying close to the rocks, as if someone purposefully put them there. She paused momentarily wondering if perhaps this was someone's regular campsite.

"Too bad," she shrugged, "You'll just have to share."

Managing to gather enough dry limbs and twigs for the night, she finally got a small blaze going. Hannah took a can of beans from her provisions and wolfed them down without bothering to warm them. All she wanted to do was sleep. Getting undressed was out of the question too. She was just too bushed, besides anyone other than animals prowling these words would more than likely be men so, lying around without clothes was not how she wanted to be caught.

"Wouldn't they just love that!" she mumbled wryly.

Catching sight of her moccasins, she shrugged, "I'll need those to run in," and finally allowed her body to free-fall back.

This only lasted as long as it took for her back to slap against the saddle. Recoiling like a spring, she sprung up to a sitting position as pain from yesterday's whipping consumed her. She couldn't hold back tears while enduring the throbbing anguish. Those deep wounds should be cleaned properly, but there was nothing to clean them with. A dip in the creek would help some, but that would just have to wait till morning. Using the carpeted valise as a cushion, Hannah pulled the rifle close and lay carefully on her side. Once comfortable, she fell into an exhausted sleep.

Later she stirred, as someone lightly touched her cheek and pushed hair back from her forehead.

"Nanny," she whispered slowly opening unfocused eyes to gaze blearily at a dark figure. "Is that you?"

The shadowy figure withdrew its hand slowly, not wanting to startle the sleeping girl. Watching as though spellbound, he inhaled sharply to keep quiet as languid eyes closed and a small smile played around the corners of her mouth.

"I've missed you Nanny," she whispered.

The silent man remained still. The girl from the stream. He'd been captivated that day by her large heavily lashed blue eyes; that even in this dim light reminded him of the colorful stones his people valued for their protective and healing powers. Should he wake her? From all appearances she needed the rest; her position hadn't changed since he'd arrived right after dark last night.

He'd chosen this site in the early afternoon and laid in a supply of dry firewood; then left to hunt supper. When he returned this girl already had a small fire going and was sleeping soundly beside it. She'd slept the night through with no idea that someone was sharing her campfire.

Rising gradually, he backed away on soundless feet watching the rise and fall of someone deeply asleep and finally decided not to wake her. It wasn't a comfortable decision;

he affirmed wondering who she was and why she was alone in the woods like this. Was she in trouble? The answer to that question had him backing away. There simply wasn't time to take on someone else's troubles.

He was now close to Traders Bluff and his work at the Empty Boot Tavern was pressing… people's lives were dependent on what he found out there. So, with one last look at the sleeping girl… woman, he'd shared last night's fire with, the shadowy figure quietly mounted his horse and headed off; with a pair of crystal blue eyes seared in his memory.

Later, Hannah again awoke to Samson's movements, only this time he was trying to pull loose. Coming awake quickly, she realized half the morning was gone, no wonder the horse was acting up. He was usually fed, watered, and roaming the pasture by this time of day.

"I meant to get a head start this morning," she groaned moving gingerly still feeling the effects of being in the saddle so long yesterday.

"I just have to get used to it," she muttered, moving slowly to attend Samson.

Grimacing painfully, she bent down to reach the canned stuff. Her back continued to hurt, but as long as she didn't lean against anything the discomfort was bearable. Remembering the dip in the creek she'd promised herself last night… it would just wait till tonight. There simply wasn't time now.

It wasn't a cold morning, so she didn't bother to rekindle the fire that must've burned itself out during the night. Instead, she squatted by its dead ashes choosing to quickly eat a can of peaches. Hannah polished these off in record time, drinking the juice to savor every drop. She decided peaches were the best food in the world. Rising and wishing for a strong cup of coffee, she began saddling Samson and repacking the gear.

She paused, a wide smile transforming her face. She had dreamed of Nanny during the night, and it had been so real, especially when the old woman had soothed her cheek and pushed the hair off her face. Tears smarted Hannah's eyes as memories of the old nursemaid coming in through the night to check on her came flooding back. Nanny's gentle pats and midnight visits had sure gone a lot further in making a child feel loved and cared for than all fancy dresses her mother was forever pushing on her.

Hannah wiped her eyes and shrugged away the past… best get a move on. Making sure nothing was left behind she spied an intricately carved wooden whistle leaning against a tree.

"Wonder where this came from," she mumbled studying the instrument closely before blowing through it.

It emitted a pleasant sound, but as her eyes scanned the ground, she noticed faint large human footprints. That meant that it wasn't the ghost of her old nursemaid touching her last night… someone… some man… because footprints that size would never belong to a woman, had been in this camp during the night.

The hairs on the back of her neck rose as a mantle of fear spread over her. Taking several deep breaths, she pulled out the rifle and began scanning the surrounding forest, looking for signs of other people… men! Precious minutes flew by as she watched and listened attentively. However, not wanting to linger, she replaced the rifle; satisfied no one else was about.

Samson snorted causing Hannah to jump nearly out of her skin. She turned to give him *what for* but bit her tongue instead. It wasn't the horse's fault she'd let some man sneak into camp. One thing for sure, he was a lot different from Hiram and Cutler if he'd been in her camp all night and all he did was touch her face.

Shaken and thoroughly disgusted with her mistake, Hannah stomped over to grab the reins and mount up; grimacing as sore muscles and back reacted painfully to another day in the saddle. She tucked the whistle into her carpet bag and headed north to follow the creek. Deeply disturbed about what could've happened last night, she realized that the God she thought had forgotten her must've been watching over her.

"Thank you, LORD," she prayed, "I promise to be more aware… It won't happen again."

As the morning turned to afternoon, Hannah reviewed the last two days trying to figure how many miles they'd traveled so far. Shaking her head in exasperation, she gave up. The territory was just too unfamiliar and after all, what was the use. There'd never be enough miles between her and the gang.

She wondered exactly where they were; close to a town… in the middle of nowhere… she honestly had no idea. However, they'd picked up a well-trod path of sorts that appeared to run alongside the creek, and since it tracked north, she decided to follow it. Hopefully, it would lead somewhere settled.

* * *

"Okay boys, if she ain't in the woods out back and she didn't go to Traders Bluff," Hiram stated looking from Cutler to Elam and then Ellis, "Where in Sam hill is she?" he questioned reaching up to carefully scratch a heavily whiskered jaw that bore the long puckered gash Hannah had given him.

The back of his head didn't look or feel any better either. Cutler wasn't a seamstress or surgeon and the haphazard way he'd pulled the skin together in order to sew up both wounds had left bloody gaps between the stitches that were now heavily scabbed over. The men sat hunkered around the fire in the cabin on the third morning following Hannah's departure.

They had searched all around the cabin and every trail leading to and from Traders Bluff without turning up a single trace of her. No one had seen her or Samson. Cutler, not trusting Pinky and Elam's assurance that Hannah was nowhere to be found, had returned to town, and prowled every saloon, livery stable, and boarding house within a day's ride, bribing and threatening anyone that didn't report her whereabouts if they knew of her.

Familiar with the outlaw's reputation for retribution, none of the townsfolk tried to stop him or even question his actions. Instead, they all stood back with bated breath, eager to provide whatever answers seemed plausible, while waiting for his foray to be over. Proprietors breathed a sigh of relief when he left, despite the upheaval he caused, as did everyone else; at least they were still alive!

He returned to Hiram's just as dawn was breaking in a foul mood, demanding that everyone get their lousy carcasses out of bed. It was time to make plans. Upon learning the futility of his search, the men sat quietly watching the fire; disbelieving that a mere slip of a girl had outfoxed them.

Pinky walked in handing around cups of coffee, before returning to get his own. He performed this quickly and quietly and settled back on Hannah's bed instead of joining the group. He had a good idea of which direction she had taken away from here, recalling the time the two of them had been deer hunting around the old Hinton homestead. She'd talked about several trails they could follow and the northerly direction of some of these.

Shaking his head nervously, he scowled. At least the jackasses around the fireplace didn't know this, and he sure wasn't about to tell them. Enjoying the power of being one up on them, he started to laugh, but covered this gaffe by taking a quick gulp of coffee to hold it back. Looking up, he found Cutler watching him with a cold intent stare.

"What's the matter kitchen boy… you got something to say?"

"Me," he sputtered, "no, nothin'… well, uh… is coffee okay boys?"

Pinky knew he was floundering like an old fish lying on a bank hoping to work his way back in the water, but there was nothing to do except try to cover.

"I probably ought to go feed the horses," he announced, rising to dump his coffee.

The quicker he got out of there the better off he'd be. However, Cutler's growled pronouncement made him jerk slightly while opening the door.

"If you know somethin' about Hannah you better tell us, cause if we find out you even have a clue where she's gone and you didn't tell us I promise you won't like the consequences," he paused to let this sink in, "dyin' won't come too soon for you… boy."

Taking a slow deep breath Pinky turned to face the man that could make his life a living hell. What he was about to say was a bald face lie, but he figured his days were probably numbered and if Hannah could get away, well at least one of them had a chance.

"I don't know where Hannah went. I never talked to her much, but I do remember her sayin' she'd like to ride one of them big riverboats down to New Orleans. It was right after we came back from that last job outside of Pine Ridge. Hiram was talkin' about gamblin' on one of them boats… that's all I know," Pinky shrugged, waiting… doing his best to maintain eye contact.

Cutler warily searched the faces of the group as if measuring their response to this revelation. Finally, after muttering some choice words about dealing with idiots, he ordered Pinky to take care of the animals. Just as the door was about to close, he yelled, "Remember what I said, Pinky boy, a slow painful death. Nobody double crosses me!"

Ellis looked at Hiram, "I remember you goin' on about them boats, but I ain't sure about anythin' Hannah said. Seems, she was always pretty quiet… she could have said somethin' like that. After all, none of us paid her much attention, well, except to bedevil her."

Elam nodded in agreement, while Hiram shook his head.

"I don't know," he began only to be interrupted by Cutler.

"Well, I do, and I don't think she's headed for no riverboat anywhere. I believe she's out in them back woods… hidin'," he paused looking defiantly from one to the other, "and I say we go search today every tree, hole, and cave we can find that a body might hide in."

Hiram readily agreed, earning a quick consent from Ellis. Elam rose and went to look out the window at the waning darkness.

"Should be light enough to see in about an hour," he stated. His twin came behind him, agreeing as Cutler began to lay out orders.

"Hiram and Elam will stay here in case she gets wind of us lookin' for her and heads this way. Me, Ellis, and Pinky will scour the woods for tracks or anythin' else that might lead to her," He paused, sending an icy gaze from one man to the other that clearly said *'don't question me'*, but Hiram asked anyway.

"Why are you takin' the kid with you? You know you can't stand him! Besides, Elam would be more help to you then he will."

Cutler cursed and spit at the fireplace, his aim coming up short of the target.

"He's goin' with me 'cause I don't trust the little bugger. I think he's lyin' about what Hannah said and I aim to poke at him till he comes clean. Sides, if he's here and she comes back, there'll be two of em to kill you this time," he finished disgustedly. "Or, do you think you could handle em both? Why, you're a real deadly man with that whip," he taunted.

Hiram flushed, his gaze sliding quickly from this detested companion to the fireplace. Not bothering to respond he threw out his next question, "Okay, let's say you don't find her," he challenged, "What's your next big idea?"

Cutler rose to glare harshly at his partner who dared to question him, before stating emphatically, "If we don't find the little tramp today then we all head for Rosedale at first light tomorrow. It looks like we've got some boats to search, and some river rats to talk to."

This statement was flung at all of them as he spun around furiously and slammed out the cabin. The three men watched the door silently, waiting for it to either fall off its hinges or vibrate itself closed. The tick of the old mantle clock rattled off several tense minutes before Elam ventured, "One of these days that door's bound to fall off."

No one responded, seemingly all lost in thought. Hiram stared in the fire recalling the day they met a man calling himself Cutler. The war had started and he and the twins, deciding to raise their status from lowly thieves to heroic saviors of the South, had gone to Richmond Virginia to help whip the Yankees. Their arrival coincided with the fevered excitement of a Confederate encampment set up on the banks of a stream called Bull Run. Anxious to join the action, they skipped the signing up process and selected a small knoll to hide behind; giving them an ideal position from which to pick off the despised invaders.

All day long, pistols and rifles fired from all directions while heavily loaded caissons supplied cannonballs filled with buckshot and shrapnel to explode on their enemies in order to kill, maim, and if nothing else, embed pieces of shrapnel deep into the opposing forces vulnerable bodies. The three friends quickly merged into the southern lines sending volleys of ammunition flying toward Yankee lines. However, it only took one bloody painful hit for Hiram to decide that no amount of heroism for southern gentility was worth his life. So, having expediently joined in the fighting without signing any papers, he decided it was time to leave.

Readily agreeing, the ever-faithful twins dragged him to the surgeon's tent where the physician explained the best thing to do would be to amputate from the knee down. There were too many fragments embedded in the flesh and with the number of wounded piling up, he couldn't take the time necessary to remove them all. Finally, he consented to take out the ones he could see and wrap the leg before instructing Ellis and Elam to leave Hiram in the makeshift infirmary.

Pretending outrage at missing the fight, the three stumbled and tripped their way around as the conflict raged on. Their efforts to escape weren't easy; obstructed by the number of injured men in various conditions crying for help while able-bodied soldiers scrambled for the best vantage point from which to annihilate their targets. Other complications included riderless horses, spooked by the noise and melee, running wildly in all directions, evading officers and a myriad of bullets that seemed to fly from all directions. Elam and Ellis half dragged, and half carried Hiram from tree to shrubbery and back to tree until finally they were clear of the battlefield.

Just as it appeared, they'd made it, their path of escape led directly in the line of a mounted Yankee captain charging rapidly in the same direction. They stopped abruptly, their gazes bouncing anxiously from each other to the stone-faced officer sitting atop a large black stallion. Jerking cruelly on the horses' reins the captain finally broke the silence speaking authoritatively, "Ho sirs, state your duty."

Hiram, the fastest thinking of the three, observed the man's sharp British accent, along with a few other curiosities such as the ill-fitting uniform that hung on a body two sizes smaller and a fresh saber slash outlining the left side of the officer's face. This long thin laceration ran from the man's left eyebrow down the entire side of his face and still oozed a slight trickle of blood to drip from his chin.

Something didn't add up here, Hiram recalled a phrase he'd once heard a British soldier yell so taking a chance he looked up, grinned conspiratorially, and said in his best mock British accent, "Ho guvnor… permission sir, to get the bloody eck out of here!"

Returning the grin, the sham officer kicked his foot free of the stirrup and hoisted Hiram up behind him.

In the same cold accented voice, he informed all, "Captain Cutler," he announced with an exaggerated salute, "Permission granted!"

After rounding up enough mounts for everyone, the four headed West, aiming for the farthest away territory where military conscription wasn't forced on anyone unwilling to voluntarily commit.

Hiram shifted in his chair and gave a noncommittal response to something one of the twins asked and returned to his musing.

As the group worked their way across the Mississippi through Missouri and then Kansas, Cutler became a valued member. He had no regard for human life or otherwise and carried himself as a man used to challenges and conflicts. Ever on the lookout for an enemy, he was an accurate shot on the draw and deadly with a knife.

He was ruled by a mind full of diabolical schemes coupled with an uncompromising conviction that all mankind owed him a living and if they didn't provide it willingly… well, he would take it by any means possible. This attitude made him a natural fit among the three individuals that felt they'd been deprived all their lives, so the three became four and while Hiram continued to give the orders, no job was carried out without Cutler's approval.

So, with plans to get rich the quickest and easiest ways possible; the Walters Gang emerged and began earning their notorious reputation for thievery, chicanery, and murder. They gambled, held up settlers headed west, robbed any bank, train or stagecoach that might contain money, and swindled lonely widows out of the deed to their properties, promptly selling them to the first offer that provided a lucrative sum. They also left a number of raped and murdered individuals behind; a testament of their callousness as well as a warning for revenge on any inclined to go to the law.

Hiram shook his head coming back to the present and muttered unthinkingly, "I rue the day we ever met that man."

"Who," Ellis asked.

"Cutler, that's who."

"You reckon Cutler's his real name," Elam questioned looking up to watch Pinky reenter the cabin.

"I don't know but remember what happened that night we tried to guess his real name?"

This time it was Ellis's turn to reminisce, "I thought sure I was done for that night."

Elam grimaced disdainfully at the thought of losing his brother while Hiram gave a chuckle shaking his head and Pinky sat up on Hannah's bed to ask Cutler's origin.

"We don't rightly know," Ellis began, "the only bit he volunteered was his escape from Newgate Prison in England some years ago followed by a ride across the Atlantic as a stowaway in the cargo section of a ship headed for America. How he came to be on the battlefield at Bull Run is anyone's guess. The same can be said for his real name. One night we was all settin' around a campfire drinkin' and started bettin' we could guess his given moniker. We all made several wild guesses… coming' up with nothin'. We was all about half drunk and laughin' our butts off and then I remembered somethin, I had seen in the label of that coat he had on that day we met him." Ellis rose to lean against the mantle before continuing.

"I proudly announced, 'I know, I know' and took me a big swig of whiskey then I said 'Captain Maxim Vincennes Rhys'. I took a bow, and everyone was laughin' well everyone except Cutler. He grabbed a fistful of my collar and hauled me up to face a gun barrel pokin' me right between the eyes and demanded to know where I heard that name. He was white as a ghost, his hands shakin' and I don't know if he was the most mad or afraid. Believe me, I was pretty scared myself… sure wasn't drunk anymore."

Pinky was totally enthralled; he couldn't imagine Cutler scared of anything mad maybe, but not scared.

"So, is that his real name?" he questioned looking from Ellis to Hiram.

"I told him it was sewed in that Yankee coat he had on that day we come across him on the battlefield. He shoved me to the ground and holstered his gun and ordered all of us to never utter that name again. He then stomped off in the dark warnin' or there'll be one less member of this gang, and then he ordered for us to make sure that bloody coat gets burned!"

"We hardly called him anything after that except '*hey Brit*', but then Hiram started callin' him Cutler again leavin' off the captain part and me and Elam gradually picked it up. He's been Cutler ever sense."

"You dang right I left off the captain bit, this is my gang," Hiram fumed, "if anybody's gonna be called Captain, it's gonna be me. Cutler may act the part, but this is my gang!"

The room was quiet following this announcement until Hiram asked one last question.

"By the way, did you ever really burn that coat?" he asked Ellis.

Ellis continued staring in the fire, but finally looked up to send a conspiratorial grin to his leader, "Nah, I figured that thing might come in right handy someday. Don't you worry I got it stashed away."

Elam cleared his throat having heard enough about their disgruntled partner and brought their conversation back to the present.

"Pinky, I sure hope you're telling the truth about Hannah."

Ellis absentmindedly grunted in agreement.

Pinky shrugged, "Why would I lie? That would serve no purpose except to get me killed," he offered lying back on the bed.

"I don't know, but for your sake I hope you're not," Hiram responded, scratching his jaw contemplatively... "You know, I think we're goin' the wrong way," he hesitated again before continuing, "I believe Hannah would head north to Jasmine and then on to Memphis," he paused briefly, "if she makes it that far she'll cross the river and head west."

"Yeah," Ellis nodded, "I agree. She's heard us talk an' knows there's too many blue bellies up there for Cutler's likin'."

"You think she's got enough wood smarts to try that... much less make it that far?" Elam asked.

"I don't know about wood smarts, but I figure she's anxious and scared enough to try," Ellis answered going over to Hiram. "You gonna tell this to Cutler?"

"I reckon I better, or there's sure gonna be a dead boy around here," Hiram replied with a heartless chuckle.

* * *

Chapter Four

Hannah sat by the campfire, rifle in hand, watching the rapidly darkening forest; her eyes darting anxiously from one shadowed object to another. She wasn't about to sleep while some man traipsed around camp tonight. Last night's mysterious visitor had taught her a lesson about the necessity of being alert at all times and sleeping with one eye open. She let out a tired sigh… if only she wasn't so doggone tired.

Today marked the end of her fourth day on the run and for the first time since leaving the cabin she actually felt preyed upon by something other than forest animals. She couldn't dispel a feeling that someone had been following her and was still out there. Samson had acted up earlier, perhaps sensing another horse or man nearby, but so far no one had shown themselves. They'd still managed to come quite a distance, thanks in part to the clear trail they'd continued to follow north. Unfortunately, she still didn't have the slightest clue where they were.

Unable to shake off her uneasiness, Hannah decided to get on with the nightly routine and opening a can of beans proceeded to fill her growling belly. She's been able to make the canned food last longer by eating only two meals a day, but it sure didn't keep the hunger at bay. If she didn't reach a town soon, it would be necessary to start hunting.

Having finished the meager supper, she arranged the makeshift bed that had worked well for the past three nights. Luckily, the stuffed carpet bag made a pretty soft cushion and kept her sore back off the dirt and bugs on the ground. Her wounds had partially scabbed over, but some were seeping and probably infected.

She needed a bath in the worst way; her hair was dirty and the smell of horse, sweat, and body odor made her sometimes wish she could stand downwind of herself. A dip in the creek could fix this and would feel mighty good, but she was too afraid to chance it. She put this off every night till the morning and every morning she put it off till the night.

"If I ever reach a town, they'll probably run me out for stinking so bad… I can't remember ever being this dirty," she frowned.

Lying down carefully, she continued watching the surrounding bushes and rocks, while keeping a firm hold on the rifle. Thoughts of a town had her wondering where exactly they were. It seemed that she and the horse had covered quite a distance, but she still didn't have the slightest clue if a town was two, ten, or twenty miles away. Hannah closed her eyes only to have them quickly pop back open, her need for sleep had been replaced by wariness for self-preservation.

This feeling of being watched had begun about mid-afternoon when she stopped to relieve nature's demanding call and saw a man half hidden behind a thicket of blackberry bushes. She wasn't sure he'd spotted her, but upon seeing him, all thoughts of anything except getting away fled her mind and she had hastily vaulted back in the saddle and made tracks. Surely, he hadn't caught up, since he appeared to be on foot. She hadn't seen a horse.

Moving restlessly, she rose to tug the saddle in front of a rock and placed the soft bag on top. Setting down, she leaned backwards slowly until her sore back was barely resting against the velvety satchel. It actually wasn't too uncomfortable, maybe she would just stay in this position for the night. She eventually dozed off, only to be awakened by the sounds of Samson thrashing about wildly.

Jerking awake, she could make out one man attempting to get on the horses back while another was creeping silently toward her. Her first conscience response was fear, as her heart began to race desperately. She wanted to get up and run, but her legs seemed to be frozen in place. Realizing this was going to get her killed or worse, she swallowed hard and silently commanded her trembling hands to position and cock the rifle.

"Hold it there," she demanded shakily, "I'll shoot!"

Her arm shook as she trained the rifle on the man stealthily creeping toward her. If looks were anything to go by, this no-good had been long without a meal and away from civilized people for a long while. His filthy clothes hung loosely on an emaciated body, showing bony knees that protruded from gaping holes in faded dungarees that stopped four inches above his ankles.

A grass string rope was all that kept the garment fastened around his waist, while a tattered vest was the only garment covering the man's chest. Long skinny bare arms were held in a position ready to grab and a face obscured by a matted dirty beard revealed sunken eyes that leered nastily, reminding her of the way Hiram always looked whenever he was intent on getting in her bed.

"Remember," she whispered, "it's your life or his. He will show you no mercy."

Having reminded herself of this, Hannah finally managed to pull her knees up and scoot into a more stable position from which to get off a good shot.

"Get away," she warned. "I'm gonna shoot and if you're not gone, by the time I count to three, one… two…"

"Naw you won't," he smirked, "'sides we just want to have a little fun. Now, be a good gal and let me have that gun 'fore you shoot yourself."

The man's approach was halted when his partner called, "Come on Harv, I finally got on the beast. Come on, mount up!"

Hannah thought her stalker was going to give up as he paused and looked at the other man, but then he turned back to her, a feral grin splitting his face and suddenly sprang forward in a huge leap. The minute he launched himself, Hannah fired, and the surprised attacker crumpled at her feet, clutching his knee and yelling.

"Elmer, Elmer, I'm shot… this little gal done gone and shot me." He writhed on the ground holding his leg and whining pitifully.

Hannah managed to stand, keeping her rifle trained on first one man and then the other.

"I told you I'd shoot, why didn't you listen?" she yelled trembling furiously.

She looked up as Elmer, still astride Samson, rode over to his companion. He looked at her nervously, holding up one hand in surrender.

"Sorry ma'am, sorry about my partner… we only wanted the horse, we weren't gonna bother you. Guess my partner kind ah went crazy. Let me get him and I promise we'll leave you alone… don't shoot no more."

He looked at her steadily before reaching down to the wounded man on the ground. "Come on Harv, git up," he ordered.

"Caint," Harv whined pitifully, "my knees smashed up… I caint stand on it."

"Stand on the other one and git up here 'fore she shoots us both."

Reaching up, Harv managed to grab the proffered hand of his companion, who jerked him to stand on one leg.

"You got to git off an' help me up," he whined giving Hannah a hateful look.

"You're just like all females… mean and untrustin'," he spat out angrily.

Hannah took a shaky step back, rifle still trained on the two men.

"I warned you I'd shoot, now like I told you get out of here…" she stopped short as the one called Elmer dismounted to stand beside his companion.

"I'm just gonna help him up… I ain't gonna do nothin' to you. We just want the horse, nothin' else. We've been walkin' for days." He ceased addressing her and talked quietly to the horse while hoisting Harv up, before springing lithely up himself.

Hannah stood watching suspiciously, still ready to shoot, as the men turned to leave. She could probably stop them if she shot the one called Elmer first, but he'd meant her no harm and she wasn't a killer. She watched the thieves and horse walk away, glad Samson hadn't acted up. She didn't want to be stuck deep in the woods with those two. They appeared to be as disreputable and wicked as the men she was running from.

Watching them lope away, she wondered what would become of Samson. She'd intended to get rid of him; just not this soon. Hannah lowered the rifle as the two men were about to ride out of sight headed back in the direction toward Hiram's hovel.

"Hey," she called loudly, causing the pair to stop and look back, "I don't know where you're headed, but you might want to stay clear of Traders Bluff. It's a little town close to Rosedale. There's a man there that owns that horse you're ridin' and he'll probably accuse you of stealin' it and hang you."

She waited for a response and was rewarded with a firm wave from the man called Elmer before he dug his heels in Samson's sides and set off in the night. Hannah breathed deeply and plopped down on top of her bag. She looked around feeling even more alone and vulnerable, as a desolate sadness settled over her.

Samson's presence had been a comfort of sorts; maybe not in the human sense, but at least another live creature on her side. Now, she was totally on her own, nothing to warn that someone was around, no fast getaway. Immediately, the situation was too overwhelming, and tears pooled and ran unchecked for a moment until Hannah took a deep breath to calm down and get a hold on her emotions.

"Can't afford to let down now," she sniffed, "feel sorry for yourself later."

She rose to stir the fire, her eyes once again searching the dark woods. There was nothing good to be said for being in the middle of a forest you didn't know, alone, and on foot. The rest of the night was spent in short restless naps that lasted long enough for Hannah to dream of being attacked by first Hiram, then Cutler, and the last time that scrawny varmint Harv. She gave up trying to sleep after that.

As the dawn began to lighten enough so a person could see where they stepped, Hannah examined her belongings, making quick decisions on which items to leave behind. The choice fell to Hiram's big saddle. There was no way she could lug that heavy thing through the woods.

"Sorry about your luck, Hiram," she shrugged and began stowing the few remaining cans of beans in the satchel.

Taking a last look around, she slipped the carpet bag's strap over her head, picked up the rifle and canteen, and started walking, continuing her trek north.

* * *

Hannah walked all that day and the next two, taking only brief intervals for much-needed breathers. As the light faded into darkness each night, she would collapse under some big bush, using her old bed pillow and valise as a cushion, and scooting back as close to its thick base as possible so the densely leafed lower branches could provide a covering. It felt safer than building a fire and sleeping in the open. Sleep became a tortured venture as she'd fall into exhausted slumbers only to be awakened by vivid dreams of being either caught, attacked, or both.

Yesterday, the trail along the creek had come to a fork, presenting the choice of veering off into the woods or continuing alongside the water. She'd decided to keep following the path by the creek; at least she was assured of having water. However, as there seemed to be no end to this track, Hannah began to wonder if she should have explored the other trail a bit, since she was lost anyway. Was she still going north? She was no longer sure.

A loud rumble signaled her stomach's empty state, but there was nothing to put in it. The last can of beans had been eaten some time ago. Gripping the rifle, she thought about hunting, but the fear of veering away from a path that surely led somewhere was enough incentive to put it off till later. Hannah stopped walking to push the bandanna off her forehead and rest her legs that quivered in exhaustion. Blinking tiredly, she started to stretch her tired shoulders but recoiled immediately; finding it too painful to expand her sore back. Instead, she straightened and tried to pull her shirt down, but it refused to give way; those lashes really weren't healing up.

Feeling excessively warm, she poured water from the canteen over her head, hoping to cool down and help clear the sluggish feeling that had persisted all day, but all this seemed to do was cloud her vision. Blinking water and grime from tired, sleepy eyes she stared around dazedly desperately trying to get her bearings. A horse's neigh or what she thought was one, echoed in her head.

"Samson?" Hannah called, straining to pinpoint exactly what she'd heard and from which direction it was coming.

The sound came again, only this time louder and closer. Remembering the man Harv, who stole the horse and still haunted her dreams, Hannah froze, standing stock still in the middle of the trail. Finally, her screaming brain got through to tired muscles and seconds before three soldiers bounded in sight, she darted off trail to hide behind a tall stand of bamboo. Breathlessly, she watched their approach and sudden halt as one of them pointed to something lying in the path.

Hannah stared with mounting trepidation, realizing the item they were talking about was Hiram's rifle. She must've dropped it. Listening attentively, she debated whether to make herself known, after all who were these men? Despite the supposition they represented law and order… well, they were still men. Judging from her experiences, men only wanted one thing from females and if they couldn't coerce her, they would force her.

"What do you say, Capt'n, sure is a nice rifle to be left in the dust like this," the soldier stated holding the weapon up for his superior to examine.

"Sure is," the burly officer replied thoughtfully, examining the gun to see if it was loaded, "too nice for the likes of Harv and Elmer White. This isn't a military issue rifle, not even from the Confederacy. Can't imagine where they'd get something like this."

"Reckon they could've stole it," asked the third man of the group.

"Could have," the captain affirmed scanning the area with a practiced eye.

"You want us to look around? See if we can scare anything up? You know they might be hiding anywhere… There's a thick cane break over there," having said this, the soldier on the ground headed for Hannah's hiding spot.

"Naw, get on back here private," the captain called, "I'm hungry and tired of chasing two yellow belly deserters that haven't the guts to protect women and children. Besides, they're weaponless and on foot, they won't last long in woods this thick with bears and snakes and other critters and even if they do, well the deep south is no place for Yankees on the run. Shoot, them secret societies of hooded man will hang 'em in a heartbeat." Here, he cackled loudly, "Don't know which is the worst… pee oohed southerners or wild crazy Injuns!"

Turning his horse, he started back in the direction they'd come, still chortling gleefully, "Guess I got myself a nice rifle though, thanks private… let's ride!" he called, spurring his horse.

Hannah slowly expelled a long uneven breath as she watched the private mount up and head after his fellow soldiers. She swayed dizzily, longing to lie down and sleep.

"Lord, I'm so tired," she mumbled, taking a staggering step forward, but there were still enough hours of daylight for travel.

"*Remember, why you're out here,*" she reprimanded herself sternly.

Keeping this in mind, she stumbled on without bothering to check the direction. It was now the simple act of putting one foot in front of the other… *keep walking… have to get away… keep walking… have to get away… keep walking.*

Along about dusk, the path she'd traveled for days merged with a rutted dirt road and Hannah, without thinking turned right to continue this seemingly endless trail. However, she hadn't gone far when her spent body gave out and she collapsed in one of the roads hollowed out ruts.

Darkness came with the sounds of Whippoorwills, cooing doves, and the nightly symphony croaking of tree frogs, but the woman lying in the dirt heard none of it. Nor did she respond to the kind man who stopped his buggy to remove what he thought was a limb in the road, but instead turned out to be a young woman. Alarmed at her fevered body and shallow breathing, he managed to get her in the carriage.

Calling out a stern, "Giddy-up," he slapped the reins on his horse's rump to set a quick pace for Jasmine.

* * *

Pinky stood outside the *Empty Boot Tavern* keeping his usual vigil for the gang, as ordered by Cutler. This watch occurred anytime they were in-house somewhere other than Hiram's cabin. His job was to stand outside, rain or shine… cold or hot, and watch for lawmen, rival gangs, or other non-desirable combatants. He was hardly ever invited inside with everyone else, which was fine with him. The women in these places were just too darned brazen he'd surmised remembering his last escapade; *"always rubbin' on you leavin' a feller smellin' like he crawled out of a perfume bottle."*

Pinky didn't have much use for gambling or whiskey and beer either. One usually took what little bit of money he could scrape together while the other burned holes in his stomach and just plain tasted bad. He'd managed to drink enough once to get good and drunk, make a big jackass of himself, and then puke his guts up all night long. That was his last go-round with that vile stuff. So, standing outside today, in the warm spring sunshine, was far more agreeable than being inside a stuffy saloon that would wreak with the smell of unwashed bodies, cheap perfume, and the ever-present fog of tobacco smoke.

Pinky leaned against the building mulling over the gang's lack of activity since Hannah left. Hiram and Cutler argued all this time about where to search for her. The question was whether to head south to Rosedale or north to Jasmine. He wasn't sure why Hiram and the twins were so dead set against Cutler's plan… they usually agreed with whatever he wanted to do, but this time was different and for some reason Pinky felt it had something to do with him.

These ponderings were suddenly interrupted when a movement at the end of the road caught his attention. A lone horse and rider came moseying slowly into town. Thinking there was something familiar about the horse, he straightened up to better examine this animal that looked an awful lot like Hiram's horse, Samson. He watched the two amble down the road and stop at the first building they came to, Taft's Tavern; a ramshackle structure that looked like it was about to fall in. The ragged rider dismounted slowly, and scanned the surroundings as though watching for someone. Apparently satisfied, he stumbled haltingly inside.

Pinky deliberated between making absolutely sure it was Samson or alerting Hiram that his horse may have shown up, after all, the continuation of this man's life was highly questionable if it did turn out to be the missing horse. Maybe he should go warn him. However, aware that he needed to stay in good with the gang, Pinky entered the Empty Boot and approached Hiram.

"What are you doin' in here?" Cutler growled impatiently. "Did I tell you to leave your post?"

"Ah, leave the boy alone," the barkeep intervened. "Let him at least wet his whistle… here boy, have one on the house."

Cutler stabbed the barkeep with an ominous glare, silently warning him to mind his own business, before kicking a chair out and ordering Pinky.

"Sit!" he commanded in a voice that brooked no arguments.

"Ain't got time right now," Pinky declared bending down close to Hiram. "I think you better come out and look at this, Hiram. I think someone just rode into town on Samson."

"You sure boy?" Hiram asked, shoving his chair back to stand and check his gun.

"As sure as I can be lookin' from here down to Taft's. I didn't go down there… thought I better come tell you first."

"Who was ridin' this horse?" Cutler demanded.

"Don't know," Pinky shrugged. "It was some scrawny fella that cain't seem to walk too good. Couldn't really tell if it was man or woman though," he finished.

"Well," Hiram turned motioning for Elam and Ellis to follow, "let's go have a look boys… could be our luck's just changed."

Cutler was out the door before anyone else, and as the others came tramping out, he was already disappearing inside Taft's. Approaching cautiously, the gang trailed Hiram's lead and stopped within a few feet of what looked like his prized horse. The sight before them was a far cry from the once spirited charger that had intimidated just about everyone except his master. Cursing Hannah vehemently, Hiram stopped and just stared at the state of the lathered, shaggy animal, standing head down at the hitching post.

Both Elam and Ellis stopped in mid step to stare at Samson, their mouths gaping in amazement while Pinky remained at the back of the group, out of sight. He wanted no part in what was sure to happen to the poor whelp that rode in on Hiram's horse. He'd like to slip away… out of town but knew there wasn't a hope in Hades of pulling that off, so he leaned wearily back against the building's rough structure watching Hiram lament over the abused horse. It was the first time he'd ever seen the gang's stalwart leader display any kind of tender emotion. It looked like he was actually going to cry while running his hands over the horse's lathered flanks and talking to it as they'd never heard him speak to a human.

Fortunately, before the scene became too embarrassing, the saloon's batwing doors were flung forcibly aside as Cutler staggered out dragging the culprit that had ridden Samson, behind him. His unrelenting grasp on the man's long dirty hair didn't let up until he had managed to fling his ragged, emaciated prisoner into the middle of the dirt road, amid the mud, leftover puddles, and ever-present piles of horse dung.

Pinky felt sorry for the man as he watched him try to crawl away, only to be brought up short by the crowd of curious patrons that were now closing in, blocking all possibility of escape. Several among them began laying odds on who would shoot the horse thief first, Hiram or Cutler. They're noisy dealings ceased abruptly as Hiram forcefully shoved through the circle, stalking to kneel over the forlorn victim.

"You got one minute to tell me how you come across this horse," he demanded, his anger evident in the shaking weapon he pressed between the man's eyes.

No one in the crowd spoke or dared breathe too loudly as they strained to hear the barely audible words the prisoner attempted to say. It was obvious that his wasted appearance went beyond simply looking depleted.

He seemed dazed and unsteady, weaving from side to side as he tried to sit up. Cutler smirked evilly and started to shove him back with his mud caked boot, but stopped when Hiram ordered Sue Ellen, one of the saloon girls, to fetch some water.

"Why in bloody kings crossin' are you…" a startled Cutler thundered, glaring intently at his partner. "You really have lost your edge Hiram," he sneered.

"Shut up," Hiram scowled impatiently. "We can't hear anything the man says if he can't talk. Besides, this is my horse were talkin' about, so leave me to it!"

Cutler executed a mock bow and stepped back without voicing a further response, but the malevolent glower he kept trained on Hiram was a sure indication that a reckoning would soon occur between these two. The crowd muttered perceptively. No one had ever seen the Brit's control of the Walters gang challenged; most just assumed that he was in command.

The onlookers silently parted once again to let Sue Ellen through with the requested mug of water. She kneeled gingerly beside the pitiful looking thief trying in vain to keep from displaying an ample amount of bosoms for all to see. Struggling to keep her full ruffled skirts out of the mud, she made a show of helping him get a firm hold on the cup before she let go.

"What's your name, sugar?" she purred in a honey dipped drawl.

"Harv, ma'am."

The crowd roared at the idea of someone addressing a barmaid as politely as 'ma'am', which prompted an offended Sue Ellen to direct a spite filled glare around the circle before announcing, "It wouldn't hurt all of you to be a little more respectful. I may serve drinks but that's all!"

Staring defiantly, she watched as some men chuckled while others shuffled in embarrassment. They all knew her word was true.

"That's enough. Get up," Hiram ordered roughly, and she rose slowly to slip behind the barkeep; still within hearing distance.

The Walters gang was up to something and she'd been paid good money to find out as much as possible without jeopardizing her life.

"Now, Haaarv," Hiram continued dragging the name out condescendingly.

Squatting down in front of the prisoner, he again positioned the pistol to bring about the best effect, "Where did you get that horse?"

Harv's eyes uncrossed as they broke focus on the gun pressing between them to look up at his inquisitor, "I... I... found it in the woods," he finally managed to stammer out.

The crowd murmured, shaking their heads with the realization that Harv had no idea who he was talking to and if he didn't come up with a better explanation than that, well, he would sure enough be a dead man before the hour was up.

Hiram shook his head slowly and cocked the pistol. It clicked with a death warning that must have convinced Harv his life was truly in danger, for immediately the words couldn't come out fast enough.

"Ho… Honestly," he sputtered, "I found him in the woods out… outside of Jasmine."

"You mean to tell me, this horse was just wanderin' in the woods, all by itself. No one around, just this animal?" Hiram queried.

He examined his prisoner closely, noting the man's dirt encrusted clothing and finally a bloodstained pant leg that stretched over a badly swollen knee.

"What happened to your knee? Did ya get that tryin' to steal that horse?" Hiram reached down and grasped the man's knee, squeezing mercilessly.

"Boy, I'm giving ya one more chance to come clean," he yelled over the painful howls of his writhing, screaming victim, "or I'm gonna pull this trigger and end your sorry life. Not one of these people standin' here is gonna stop me. You see we all hate horse thieves."

"I took the horse from some gal camped in the woods," Harv screamed in agony.

The pressure on his knee ceased immediately as Hiram realized what the man had just revealed. He pulled his gun back slowly, glancing up first at Cutler and then his other partners. A low mumble once again spread through the circle of onlookers as they watched the scene and tried to figure out the significance of the victim's last statement.

Harv continued moaning in pain and again tried to scoot away as Cutler, along with Elam and Ellis squatted around him. These efforts were halted as his backward crawl led him smack into Ellis who laid a firm hand on his shoulder warning, "Be still boy, we still got some talkin' to do."

"Everybody, go back to your own business. There'll be no hangin' today. We're just gonna talk to this… err… Harv and then we're gonna see if Doc's sober enough to check out that knee," Cutler announced dispersing the crowd with these words along with his usual stony eyed glare.

Hunkering down in front of the man still in question, he eyed his partners viciously.

"Now, I'm gonna ask the questions," he spat out in a tone that dared any of them to object.

"Where…" he asked honing his attention directly on Harv, "did you come across this girl and that horse?"

Harv must've decided that no one was going to come to his defense and these men were set to kill him if he didn't say something they wanted to hear.

He began slowly, "I was being chased out of Jasmine by three blue bellies that was danged determined to throw me back in the stockade. So, I started runnin' through them woods, hidin' in trees, under bushes… anywhere to get away. A few days ago, I come across this girl ridin' that horse and followed her all day. Then, when darkness came, I snuck in her camp and took the horse." Here, he paused looking from one of his guards to the other before continuing, "That's the truth, so go ahead beat me, kill me… I reckon at this point it don't matter… Just get it over with," he whined piteously.

Everyone ignored the man's attempt for sympathy as Hiram continued the questions, "That girl tell you her name?"

"Naw, and I sure didn't ask, 'specially after she shot me," Harv replied disgustedly. "All I was tryin' to do was get a can of peaches and that skinny, red headed female about shot my leg off."

"You sure that's all you was tryin' to do?" Ellis snickered.

Any further comments were cut off as Cutler directed a discouraging stare his way before prompting one final answer from Harv.

"Did this girl say anything else?" He waited impatiently as Harv appeared to think about his response.

Finally, a dejected Harv muttered, "Yeah, she told me not to come to this town, 'cause some man would say I stole his horse." He shook his head forlornly, "I figgered she was lyin'."

The four men surrounding Harv rose to look at each other in confirmation. They knew for sure he was talking about Hannah and she was headed north to Jasmine. Their self-proclaimed leader took command of the group.

"Let's go, we got some plannin' to do," he stated then without bothering to see if anyone followed, headed for the Empty Boot.

He stopped long enough to peer searchingly up and down the muddy road until spotting his target, then bellowed a command that brooked no argument.

"Pinky, get your sorry carcass down here and take care of Hiram's horse, then get back to your post." Pinky moved to carry out the order, stopping beside the now forgotten Harv still lying in the road.

"Best to move out of the way," he addressed the man. "When I come back from the livery I'll see if Doc's able to see ya."

Harv nodded his response and Pinky hurried over to Samson. Leading a much quieter version of the once high-spirited steed. He headed to the livery reflecting on everything he'd just learned; his emotions careening from one extreme to the other. He was glad Hannah had gotten away. She deserved her freedom, but sadly that freedom would be short-lived 'cause from now on, she would be hunted like an animal or least way as long as Cutler was alive.

Chapter Five

Jasmine, Mississippi

Dr. George Carter or just plain Doc to his patients, brought the galloping horse to a halt outside a weathered farmhouse shouting, "Maude, Maude Sharp, open that door and get out here. I need some help… fast!"

Chickens scattered in a flurry of squawking protests and flapping wings while Clyde, a speckled coon dog, roused from his nap on the porch to set up a baying howl announcing a visitor. The front door was flung open and a woman with dripping wet hands emerged to stand on the porch and shush the howling dog. She, at first glance, presented a formidable appearance evident in her tall full-figured build, coupled with a serious face bearing the beginning lines that accompany maturity and life experiences.

However, this impression could be quickly dispelled as most people were treated to her gentle nature, quick wit, and laughing brown eyes. Still, she could at times come across with a no-nonsense attitude, which was obvious today as she hurried across the porch, while scolding the careworn man descending from his squeaky carriage.

"Land sakes, what a ruckus!" she exclaimed wiping her hands on an apron that covered her from shoulders to knees.

"I imagine everyone from here to town knows you need help after that caterwaulin' fit," she quipped coming around to peer inside the buggy, "My word, what ya got there? Is he dead?"

"Naw, not yet, but she's gonna be and soon if we can't help her," Doc answered rubbing his face wearily while rounding the buggy. "I don't have time to take her to my office. I'm on my way to the Hampton place now and this is making me late. Lenore's in labor. Can I leave this one here and get you to look after her… leastways till I get back?"

Maude peered inside the carriage at the tall dirty person now lying across the worn leather seat.

"You mean that's a girl?" she asked taking in the filthy dungarees and short cropped hair. "Never seen a female with hair that short," she stated looking at Doc Carter quizzically.

A weary Doc shook his head in annoyance, "Will you help me? If not, I got to go, but if this young woman dies before I can tend her it'll be on your head." He emphasized this last point with a stern glare at Maude and then turned to climb back in the buggy.

"Hold on, George Carter," she ordered reaching in to pull the prone figure to a sitting position. "Have you ever seen the day when I turn a body in need away from my door?" she asked frowning furiously.

Doc Carter sighed with a shamefaced grin, "Naw Maudie, I knew you wouldn't, which is one reason why I came here. That… and well, you're the closest person I could call on, except for Harriet Collier."

Maude grimaced sourly at the mention of this name and directed Doc to push the front door open wider.

"So, we won't have to deal with it once our hands are full," she explained as he returned.

Grasping their unconscious patient under the arms and knees, they slowly made their way inside. "We'll put her in that backroom off the kitchen," she instructed.

"My, but she's a tall drink of water, for a girl," Maude remarked straightening the legs of their patient now lying on the bed.

She stood back and watched silently while Doc performed a quick examination, checking for heartbeat, peering into eyes, and taking other precursory assessments. Straightening up, he motioned for Maude to approach the other side of the bed.

"Help me get this shirt off of her. She's burning up with fever. Let's see if there's any wounds that could cause this."

"These clothes will never come clean," Maude stated reprovingly as she unbuttoned the dirty shirt, "best to just throw them away."

"I'm not worried about her clothing," Doc replied wryly, lifting his patient so Maude could pull it from beneath her. "By the way, we need some scissors," he continued noticing the cloth wound tightly around the woman's chest.

He didn't bother to comment on this, after all throughout the past thirty years of doctoring he'd seen many types of devices people used to disguise their identities; this was one of the most common.

"Hold her up a little more Doc," Maude instructed, "this shirt is stuck. Must be caught under her," she finished jerking firmly on the cloth that tore away to reveal several seeping pus-filled wounds. "Oh, my word," she exclaimed, removing the shirt, and stepping back in dismayed silence.

Doc Carter peered over the patient's shoulder and shook his head in disgust.

"No wonder she's running such a fever. Looks like someone tried to beat her to death. Turn that cover back while I got her up here; no need to ruin your good quilt," he finished before laying the young woman back.

While Maude obeyed, he stepped back, scratching his chin in thoughtful contemplation. Retrieving the scissors, Maude finished undressing the still unconscious patient, who moaned pitifully before lapsing back into a state of oblivion.

"Must be painful," she remarked snipping the chest binding up the middle.

It sprang apart instantly, displaying a well-developed bosom.

"Goodness… now, why would a young woman want to go and hide something like this," Maude wondered out loud.

Doc Carter shook his head, fixing his helper with a sardonic grin, "Has it been that long Maudie since the young bucks wouldn't leave you alone? You know how crazy my species can act over the female anatomy."

He rolled the young woman over to look at her back mumbling about the disgusting behavior of some men. Stuffing a pillow behind her, Doc took a closer look at the seeping wounds, noting numerous scars and faded bruises.

"Maudie, I'm pretty sure she's feverish from the infection in all of those wounds." He shook his head, pacing beside the bed before walking out. "I'll be right back," he called over his shoulder.

Maude pulled a sheet up over the young woman and went to get a basin of water and some cloths. Returning to the room, she began to gently wash away some of the sweat and grime that appeared to cover every inch of the body. After all, she didn't need doc's instructions on how or when to wash a dirty body up, especially when they were lying in one of her beds.

Doc returned carrying his medical satchel, along with an old dirty carpet bag.

"Here," he held up the leaf and dirt encrusted bag, "I guess this holds the few belongings she was carrying. I had to practically pry it from her grip, even in the state she's in."

He set the bag at the end of the bed and moved to open his satchel. From this, he retrieved a bottle of carbolic acid, a small container of laudanum, and a role of bandages.

Sighing regretfully, he looked at Maude explaining, "I hate to leave you like this, but I have to get over to the Hampton's before that baby arrives without me. I know I can trust you to clean those wounds and care for this girl till I get back. Give her a drop of that laudanum if she comes to. It'll help her rest better and from the looks of her, I'd say she could use some rest."

Maude laid down her washcloth and followed the beleaguered doctor out with assurances not to worry; she'd done this before. Giving one last wave, she watched his retreating buggy head down the road and quietly shut the door. Returning to the sick room, she stood looking at the unconscious young woman; observing her pale complexion that accentuated the heavy dark circles and long brown lashes that defined her closed eyes. A smattering of freckles across a small straight nose and dull red chopped off hair along with a long lanky body, badly in need of sustenance, completed the rest of this scraggly looking female.

"Well, young lady," Maude sympathized shaking her head regretfully, "we got our work cut out… hope you can stand it. I'm afraid you're going to hurt before we're through, but I know you'll feel a lot better afterward."

Retrieving her cloth, she continued cleaning the patient, speculating on who could have treated her so badly.

"Humph," Maude exclaimed out loud. "More to the point, who are you, how far have you come, and will someone be following?"

* * *

The tall stranger entered the Empty Boot and took a seat against a back wall providing him a full view of both doorways leading in and out of the building. There was nothing unusual about his appearance, in fact he blended in well with all the other indolent miscreants that frequented the tavern; a cross between river pirate and cattle rustling stage robber. However, if one looked closer they'd notice alertness in the eyes that quickly absorbed everything around him, seemingly weighing its significance. He'd been hanging around for the last few days, surreptitiously watching the Walters gang.

Slouching casually in his chair, he waited patiently for everyone to troop back in from watching the questioning of that poor sap outside. It was winding down when he left, so it wouldn't be long now. From the sounds of things, his patient observations were about to pay off, the Walters gang was getting ready to move again. Hopefully, the barmaid had gleaned more information from her position at the front of the crowd than he had been able to ascertain from the back.

It couldn't happen any too soon for him! This venture east of the Mississippi left him feeling displaced, too many people, too crowded. Pulling his hat a little lower, he sipped beer and watched the four outlaws stomp through the doors to take chairs close by. Leaning as far over the table as he could without looking obvious, he listened as the one called *Cutler* laid out just who would be leading the gang and where they were heading.

He was surprised that no one offered any suggestions or objection to the new orders, especially after the arguments they'd carried on for the past week. However, this silence was short-lived when one gang member rose quickly, demanding loudly.

"Why cain't I go to Jasmine with Elam, instead of Pinky?"

Cutler rolled his eyes in exasperation before slamming down the mug of beer he was drinking, sloshing the warm suds across the table to splatter Hiram.

"Who the dickens is runnin' this outfit?" he roared glaring from Ellis to Elam and then to Hiram.

"I always thought Hiram was the runnin' it," Elam ventured guardedly, "leastways he has been… uh, 'til… uh, now." His words trailed off lamely as he intercepted a blazing glower from Cutler.

"Guess I'll go get Pinky and saddle up," he grabbed his hat turning to leave, before halting to catch the self-appointed leader's next words.

"Remember, you're to ride into that town all nice and respectable like. Check with the sheriff, doctor, bordin' houses and taverns to see if anyone's seen or got word of Pinky's sister that up and ran away from home; and no getting' drunk and no women," he ordered.

"Ya sure know how to take the fun out of the man's life, don't ya?" Hiram drawled sarcastically.

This statement elicited a derisive snort from their aggravated leader as he leaned close to Hiram and Ellis to inform them in a low contemptuous tone, "Yeah, I sure do and I know how to run this gang. Look at ya… you've gone soft first lettin' that naggin', whinin' excuse for a wife dupe ya about them jewels and then you let a miserable, skinny wench of a girl almost kill ya! Ya can't even protect yourself, always squallin' about 'my leg; my leg hurts so bad… I cain't go on this raid boys'."

Cutler delivered the last part of his speech in a mocking tone that let both men know his respect for Hiram was long gone. He straightened up slowly, glancing sharply between his two companions, to deliver a final warning,

"Now, if I have to ride to kingdom come to do it, I'm gonna find Hannah and after I get them jewels I'm gonna make her bloody sorry for what she did to you Hiram and for runnin' off. What I want to know is if y'all are goin' with me, and if you are," he jabbed his finger at each man, "let there be no more questions about who's givin' orders or who's in charge of this gang."

Having said this, Cutler stood silently watching his two partners… waiting for a '*yea*' or '*nay*' to his declaration. Receiving a surly, but affirmative nod from each, he headed to the door to retrieve Elam and Pinky, and with everyone assembled he recapped the plan.

"We all know blue bellies are still patrolin' everywhere. And, for reasons I don't have to say I can't go around them. So, till we know where Hannah's headin' its best if I stay put here and Hiram may as well stay too. You boys," he nodded his head toward the three other gang members, "will be doin' all the scoutin' and searchin' out leads till we get a clear direction. For starters, Elam, you, and Pinky will go to Jasmine, find out what you can and report back here. If," he paused to glare at Pinky, "this sniveling little rat screws this up in any way Elam, I promise Ellis is a dead man. So, ya better make sure and bring him back with ya," he paused again then added coldly, "dead or alive! Oh, and make note of how many Yankee boys are hangin' around there."

Cutler finished rehashing the plan and addressed Ellis with a cruel sneer, "Now, see why ya can't go with Elam... you are valuable assurance," he saluted with an evil cackle before disappearing outside.

The four remaining partners looked from one to the other, silently acknowledging the truth.

"Ya know," Ellis offered, "He means to kill all of us off before this is over."

"Yeah, and that's why we gotta watch each other's back," Hiram breathed heavily, "And once we know for sure where Hannah is, we kill that Bloody Brit first," he stated.

"Get this Pinky," he continued, "No screw ups. You do what Elam says and get back here... ya got that?"

Pinky stood quietly, scratching a speck on the table. He looked up long enough to voice his consent while silently rejoicing at finally having an opportunity to get away for good. The stranger at the back table quietly finished his beer, grimacing at its taste. At least he didn't have to worry about getting drunk.

The patrons often complained about watered-down whiskey, apparently the proprietor watered down the beer too. He rose quietly, approached the tavern girl, and dropped a dollar and a note in her hand with instructions on when to meet him, before heading out the door. At least he'd have some noteworthy details for his partner when he caught up to him, but that would be for a while yet; best hang around here, see what else he could find out.

The barmaid had been a real helpful and their meetings in the barn easy to arrange since her pa supposedly worked there but laid around in a drunken stupor most of the time. Her excuse for checking on him provided ample time to impart information, for a hefty fee of course. He didn't mind paying though, her need for money was obvious, especially if she carried out the plans she'd revealed to him. He'd consider it an honor to help anyone be rid of this town.

As for him, such places had been common temporary residences for the past two months as he trailed the Walters gang from their last raid on the Brazos River to this current location; a hole in the wall town comprised of similar wanted miscreants who, despite their own illicit lives, had the nerve to look down on him. After all, he was a half breed and even lowlifes as disreputable as Queenie wouldn't rent him a room.

He shrugged it off; all too familiar with this brand of disdain. He was lucky this girl didn't seem to feel that way. Any other time, he might try to get a little friendly, but now wasn't the time for complications. Besides, while she was pretty... that yellow hair and green eyes could probably turn many a man's head; but he couldn't shake the image of a young woman sleeping in the forest with fiery red hair and eyes the color of the eyes the color of sky stones.

She haunted his dreams.

* * *

April 11, 1866, Jasmine, Mississippi

She had to move, had to get away from the fire. Why was she lying so close to the flames? Got to get back... someone help me! She sensed a presence standing close and tried to reach out to them, but her arms wouldn't budge. She was trapped!

"Help," she rasped twisting feebly, "hot... fire so hot... got to get away."

A gentle hand soothed her shoulder and she momentarily ceased trying to flee; wondering if perhaps she had run all the way back to her old home and nanny was beside her.

"Nanny," she whispered pleadingly.

Maude continued sponging the patient down as the clock in the parlor struck one and the early morning silence was interrupted by the onslaught of another spring storm; the third one this week. She shuddered at the fierceness of the wind that slashed rain against the window accompanied by an ominous growling thunder. It seemed to go on forever, rolling slowly from one side of heaven to the other. Oh well, storms always did seem to carry on worse in the middle of the night; much like fevers or any other sickness for that matter.

Once again, the young girl began to move restlessly in a feeble attempt to get up.

"No," she yelled in a panicked voice, "No Cutler… Hiram… not dead." Her legs moved restlessly as though trying to walk off the bed, "go… got to keep walking… hot," she finished in a hushed voice.

Finally, after several episodes of this, she lapsed into an exhausted silence. Maude shook her head worriedly and continued her gentle ministrations. This was the fourth night since Doc Carter had dropped off this woebegone stranger, and the fever that burned through the thin body still continued its relentless rage. Exchanging her now dried cloth for a freshly soaked one, she laid it across the girl's forehead and sank wearily into the rocking chair beside the bed, hoping the willow bark tea the girl had finally swallowed would do some good. She leaned back sighing anxiously.

There was something about this girl that brought to mind things long buried from Maude's past; things that stirred her heart with a desperate need to help this girl if she could. It was this feeling that brought to mind the only never-failing source of comfort and hope a body had and with a reassuring sense of peace and faith she began to pray.

"Dear Lord, we're all here by your grace and we know the power of life and death is in your hands. I've done everything I can for this girl and well, I'm asking you to take over. I don't know where she's from or what she's done, but it looks like she's had a hard life from the looks of that back and no meat on her bones. I know you're a merciful God and only you know if she's ready to come to you, and if she's not I ask you to give her a chance. I don't think she's had much of one for a long time, but if you don't take this fever away, she sure don't have one now. I believe your will is righteous and you can do all things, so I give her to your care and ask this in your… pre-ci-ous… name…" Her prayer gradually faded to gentle snores as concern gave way to her tired bodies demand for sleep.

Maude's next conscious thought was to wonder what that old coon dog was barking at in the middle of this storm, but as Clyde continued to howl she came fully awake to realize it was morning, the storm was over, and that was a sure enough warning someone was outside. Maude yawned widely, rising stiffly from the chair, and headed to the parlor.

"Land sakes," she muttered peering through the window, "just what I need Harriet Collier!"

Opening the door, she crossed her arms and leaned against the jamb, blocking its entrance. Maintaining a stern face, she addressed the visitor in a tone that conveyed now wasn't the time for idle gossip.

"Harriet," Maude nodded her head in a curt greeting, "What brings you out today?"

"Well, that's a fine howdy do," the arrogant self-important woman grumbled dismounting hastily from her carriage.

"Aren't you even gonna ask me in out of this muddy yard?" she grimaced, gesturing offensively at the mud puddle she had stepped in.

Between frustrated swipes at some mud that splattered her velvet skirt she continued, "The least you could do is offer me a drink of water or even a cup of tea after I come all this way to give you a message."

"A message huh," Maude snorted turning, "more like a nasty half-truth that'll hurt somebody's feelings. Stay here, I'll be back with some water for that spiteful tongue of yours," she ordered reentering the house.

Hurrying to the kitchen she filled a cup of water and turned to find her visitor hadn't stayed in place after all.

"Should've known you wouldn't carry out a simple request Harriet," she stated holding out an old-battered tin cup. "Here's your water, now what's this message?"

Harriet took the cup and simply held it as she stared at the woman in front of her with narrowed eyes and a suspicious steely glare.

After several moments of silent scrutiny she asked, "Are you after Doc Carter? Why's he sending messages to you?"

Maude's face registered first shock and then indignation at the absurdity of this question.

"Harriet Collier, what are you talking about? Don't you go spreading any rumors about me and Doc," she warned.

Harriet continued, ignoring Maude's words. "You know I set my cap for Doc. He's as good as spoken for," she spat out, "and now you're trying to come between us!"

Maude's indignation turned to laughter as she watched the outraged jealous woman vibrate angrily. Poor Harriet, she'd been after Doc since coming to Jasmine a year ago. She'd dogged his steps, cornered him at town socials and church and after all this time, still hadn't captured the wily physician. Somehow, he'd managed to evade her ceaseless efforts.

Maude watched in silent amusement, tempted to play this out, but knew in the end it would only bring trouble for Doc. She was suddenly shocked from these thoughts by a splash of cold water that landed across her bosom and onto her face.

"My word Harriet," she gasped realizing her amused response had unwittingly baited the jealous woman's ire, prompting her to lose control and fling the contents of the cup at her assumed rival.

Maude couldn't decide whether to shake some sense into the silly woman or run her out of the house with the frying pan. However, she took a deep breath and stepped back, deciding that neither was a sensible option; one of them had to at least try and act like an adult. She wiped her face and was about to address Harriet's concerns regarding whatever message Doc might have sent when a weak urgent cry from the patient in the back room filled the strained silence that had fallen between the two women.

Harriet's face changed rapidly from wrath to surprise as she pointed to the back room. "You have someone staying here?" she asked forgetting her earlier anger at the chance of finding something new to talk about.

Maude moved to stand between Harriet and the back of the house. She felt protective of the girl in that bed. There seemed to be a fearful despair that tortured her, making rest or sleep impossible. She was running away from something or more likely someone and there wouldn't be any chance of escaping unnoticed with Harriet blabbing her whereabouts all over town. Unfortunately, the town gossip wasn't to be deterred and quickly darted around the obstacle blocking her path to rush toward the back room.

"Harriet Collier, you are the nosiest, most disrespectful woman I've ever had the misfortune of knowing," Maude exclaimed highly exasperated.

Harriet paid no heed to Maude's tone, instead asking, "What's the matter with them are they sick; sounds like they're hurting something fierce." She glanced back over her shoulder and stopped, "Well, are you going to just stand there? Sure, sounds like they could use some help."

Throwing her hands up in surrender, Maude headed for the back room. Rounding the bed, she picked up the previously discarded rag to once again sponge down the patient. Harriet leaned over the bed closely studying its occupant.

"What's wrong with this boy?" she asked quietly, "you don't reckon its smallpox do you?" Here, she began backing away from the bed, fearful of its contagion.

"No Harriet, it's not smallpox. He's got some cuts on him that's infected. Apparently, he's not been taking care of himself," Maude replied noticing her patient's face and arms were considerably cooler.

She watched Harriet hover half in and half out the door, torn between self-preservation from sickness and her insatiable urge to find out all she could about the entire situation.

Finally, curiosity won out and the nosy woman blurted out, "Who is he? Where did he come from?"

Maude had already decided she would reveal as little as possible about this person to anyone, especially someone like Harriet, and well… if she thought this was a boy, all the more better.

"This is my nephew… my sister's boy. He showed up here the other day, sick as a dog." "*Lord forgive me that little lie,*" she prayed inwardly.

"How'd he get here?" Harriet asked coming back in the room. "I know he didn't come in on the stage and there's not been any one new around town."

Maude sent the woman a sardonic glance before asking, "How do you manage to keep an eye on so many places? It's a good thing you don't have a family to care for, cause either they'd die of neglect for care, or you'd die from exhaustion between cooking and cleaning and nosing."

Sighing in exasperation she answered Harriet's earlier question, "I guess he walked all this way, since he wasn't riding a horse. And with him being so sick that's all I know. By the way, didn't you say doc sent me a message? Rest assured it will pertain only to my nephew here… nothing else. So unruffle your feathers and tell me the message. You got no cause to be jealous of me and Doc!"

Harriet looked somewhat ashamed after Maude's last statement but offered no hint of apology for earlier accusations.

"Oh well," she continued haltingly, "he said to tell you he'll be by this evening. It appears Lenore Hampton had trouble birthing this last baby, but Doc brought her through it. I think he's amazing," she beamed.

"Yeah, Doc's a good man," Maude replied, "but I believe most of the credit goes to the good Lord. After all, doctors are human just like you and me. They just got a little more book learning than us, that's all. The good Lord's the one in charge of whether we live or die."

She moved to usher Harriet out of the room and toward the front door.

"Now, we need to come out of here and let this boy rest. I believe his fever is starting to come down."

Finally, she got Harriet out of the house and into her carriage without any more questions, but the determined gossip wouldn't leave without issuing a couple of final warnings.

"I'll be back to check on your nephew," she trilled flicking the reins on the horse's rump.

Maude shook her head ruefully. She had expected that one and after their earlier exchange should have expected Harriet's next one, but it still caught her off guard, "Remember this, I'm keeping my eye on you Maude Sharp. You better not be trying to spark Doc Carter."

Maude was again taken back by Harriet's suspicions, but as earlier surprise turned into humor and she leaned against the door laughing heartily.

"Just wait till Doc hears this," she told the old hound, ruffling his floppy ears.

* * *

Hannah surfaced to consciousness slowly, quietly sensing her surroundings. She touched the object on which she was lying wondering what it was. It felt like something she hadn't laid on in a very long time. There was certainly nothing this soft in the woods or in her corner at Hiram's either. She listened intently hoping to pick up some sound that would indicate her whereabouts; afraid to open her eyes; for fear this sense of comfort and peace would disappear. However, it vanished immediately as she picked up the subdued voices of a man and woman's conversation, which from their words sounded like they were talking about her.

"I tell you Doc, I didn't think that fever was ever going to break. It seemed like she was going to burn right to a crisp. I never felt so helpless in all my life. I reckon it was just turning it over to the Almighty God… that's what took care of it; should've done that in the first place."

"Now, Maudie," he stated reaching over to pat her hand, "you did a good job in there. That girl would have surely died without your care. I guess between my carbolic acid, your willow bark tea, and the good Lord, we fixed her up pretty good; a remarkable combination, wouldn't you agree? Why, between the three of us we could take care of a lot of things around here," he finished with a rascally grin.

"Humph," Maude replied, "I know one thing we couldn't take care of."

"Oh yeah, what's that?" Doc looked up from cleaning his spectacles to peer curiously at his longtime friend.

"Harriet Collier, that's what... imagine her warning me about sparking you," she stated indignantly.

"Why Maudie, I'd be right honored. How long have we known each other... since third grade if I remember right?" he paused in mischievous consideration, "I guess we're old enough for sparking by now. Besides, you're a lot prettier than Harriet Collier will ever hope to be," he grinned taking in her tall full figure, the dark hair that now showed flashes of gray and a plain yet gentle countenance that had always been attractive and dear to him.

"Poor Harriet can't hold a candle to you," he tsked teasingly.

"Land sakes George Carter," she yelped in alarm, "don't you be carrying on any such thing and certainly not in front of Harriet; that little pea hen would go into conniption fits. She's already flung water in my face, no telling what she'd do next."

"I wish I'd seen that," he chuckled ignoring his friend's outrage. "Sorry I missed that little to do, but I guess you're right. We better behave ourselves." He sobered instantly, "Seriously though, I wish she hadn't found out about that young woman in the other room. I guess I wasn't thinking too clearly by sending her out here. It'll be all over town by now."

"I agree, but it's okay for the present. She believes my nephew wandered in. You'll have to vouch for my story. I hated to lie, but I believe that girl had a bad life and needs a chance for a better one. Something about her touches my heart," she paused to look at Doc determinedly, "and I reckon if she'll let me, I aim to help her."

Doc's teasing mood faded as he gravely watched his determined friend, "You sure about this Maude?" he asked anxiously. "We don't know anything about this girl and from what you tell me, she's running from some kind of trouble. She may have even killed a man or leastways helped someone kill him."

"Well of course I intend to ask her some questions," Maude responded crossly, "like… like where came she from, and uh … what was she doing in them woods and so forth…"

"And I guess you think she's going to just tell you the truth?" Doc challenged, not waiting for her to finish her statement.

Whatever answer Maude was set to give never made it out as a loud thump followed by the crash of shattering pottery resounded throughout the small house. Running into the back room, they found the bed empty, and a weak trembling patient crumpled on the floor amidst a broken pitcher and basin that had been knocked off the table.

"My word," Maude exclaimed rushing to the girl's side. "What are you trying to do kill yourself? Here, let's get you back in bed.

Why didn't you just call for help?" The questions kept coming as she and Doc resettled their patient.

Once settled, the girl began to cry silently; her tears flowing back to soak into the matted dirty hair that stood around her head in dull red peaks like a tarnished crown. It presented a pitiable picture, which drove Maude to reach down and gather the forlorn figure in her arms and begin rocking lightly.

Doc watched concerned that Maude's motherly nature was keeping her from seeing any possible danger that could be at the root of this situation. He'd seen a lot of desperate and often dangerous people during the war and now that it was over there seemed to be even more of them; some running from family, some running from the law. This young woman was possibly running from both.

Biting back concerned comments, he chose to let it go for the moment and decided to examine his patient's back while it was so conveniently exposed. Gently raising Maude's voluminous gown, which swallowed this girl, he scrutinized a back that displayed several years of whiplash scars along with the now rapidly healing sores that would likely add new inventory to the already crowded cross-hatched flesh. One thing for certain, she'd sure been through a rough time. He lowered the gown and stepped back as Maude laid the now quiet girl back on the bed.

Maude continued her ministrations; holding the patient up while she drank, fluffing her pillows, and tucking the cover in securely. At last, seemingly satisfied she sat down in the chair beside the bed.

"What on earth were you trying to do young lady?" the question seemed to burst out impulsively, "don't you realize how sick you've been?"

The patient's eyes darted from the woman in the chair to the man standing on the other side of the bed as though gauging their trustworthiness. Several tense moments passed before she started to speak, but then stopped abruptly.

At last, she hesitantly asked, "Where am I?"

Doc watched her intently as he introduced himself and revealed how he found her and brought her to the lady in the chair.

"This is Maude Sharp and she's nursed you through a serious fever caused by them sores on your back."

He noticed color flood her paper white face when he mentioned her back but decided to venture on. A little embarrassment never hurt anybody.

"Now," he continued, "we can tell you've been treated badly, and I'd say it's a sure bet you're running away from someone. However, you won't be going anywhere for a while… you're simply too weak and run down, so you may as well not try to get out of this bed' till you get a little more strength… eat some of

Maude's good cooking. Now, I'm going to hush up and let you tell us some things we need to hear; for example, where are you from and do you want to go back…"

The young girl looked horrified at this prospect and vehemently shook her head no.

"Okay," Doc continued holding up his hand to stop the protests.

"How old are you, and most important," he paused to make sure she was looking him in the eye; "did you kill or help kill anyone?"

"Doc Carter," Maude interrupted anxiously, "do you have to start in on her so soon? The poor things just woke up. Give her time to get some strength before you start hammering away at her." She reached over and took the girls hand, squeezing it reassuringly.

Doc snorted impatiently, "See here, suppose someone is coming after her, we need to know if it's an angry pa, upset husband or even the law. Granted, we'll help if we can, but we've got to know all the facts about this girl."

He rubbed his whiskered face wearily and plopped down on the foot of the bed. Crossing his arms over his chest, he leaned back clearly indicating that he expected to sit there until all his questions were answered satisfactorily. The young woman stared at Maude and then Doc. Sensing Maude's gentleness; she sent a brief half smile her way. However, her expression became more guarded when she looked at the doctor.

Clearing her throat, she began hesitantly, "I… I defended myself… I don't think… I'm pretty sure I haven't killed or helped kill anyone. Now, I'm not going to tell you my name or anything else about me. The less you know the better off you'll be. And, as soon as I'm able I'll be leaving here, and you'll never see me again."

Having said this, the young girl's strength seemed to evaporate, and she closed hollowed eyes, exhaustion driving her to sleep. Maude and Doc exchanged disquieted looks and left the room.

"Maybe I should take her to my office," Doc muttered, "leastways you'd be safer," he said retrieving his medical bag.

This prompted a heated discussion over Maude's safety, Doc's overprotectiveness, which Maude insisted he had no right to assume, and an independent woman's stubbornness that could quite possibly result in serious injury or even her demise.

The two old friends stood regarding each other obstinately, refusing to give in. At last, Maude turned and headed to the kitchen, that girl would need a hearty broth when she woke up. She could feel Doc's solemn stare and waited for his objections to continue. Unable to stand the lengthening silence any longer she whirled around and demanded irritably,

"Well, let's hear it. We haven't got all night and I know you have plenty to say, so spit it out."

Doc paced quietly before stating, "I sure brought you a mess of trouble this time." He stood still for a moment then asked, "You reckon she was telling the truth in there… you believe her don't you?"

"I do," Maude replied unequivocally.

"Why? How can you just take her word… 'cause those stripes on her back? It's clear she's in some kind of trouble. You want that trouble to come here, because from what she just said it sure enough will. Somebody's going to come after her."

Maude allowed Doc's rant and bluster to wind down before she responded.

"You remember when we were kids and how you'd find me crying and hiding in that old apple tree on your property, well… that usually happened right after my daddy beat either me or mama with an old riding crop. Oh, he was smart about it… always striking the body where no one could see any marks… all loving husband and father in public," her words trailed off as bitter memories long tucked away surged forward.

"Why?" Doc asked quietly.

"I don't know," Maude answered, "oh, he'd come up with some reason, mama smiled at some man in town or I needed to be taught lessons in obedience. Best I can figure, he was mean and liked to hurt things that couldn't hurt him back," she finished covering her eyes as though to block out the horrible recollections.

She took a considering look at Doc before resuming her story, "I once told your ma about my pa's cruelty. She said that wasn't her business. Said some men are like that and us women just have to take our punishment if we want to keep a roof over our heads."

Pausing to light the cook stove Maude continued resolutely, "I never told another soul about this till now. I figured that if the upstanding Mrs. Carter thought it was okay then everyone else would too."

Doc Carter winced shamefully at his mother's behavior. However, it wasn't surprising. He knew firsthand that she was devoid of human understanding and warmth; a misplaced society minded female concerned too much with money and social appearance. How she came to marry a country doctor like his pa was beyond his knowledge or imagination. Sighing regretfully, Doc listened as Maude carried on.

"Mama and me, we didn't take matters in hand to end our suffering like it appears that girl in the other room did, but we weren't sorry when that old bull stomped pa in the ground. If you remember, we didn't shed nary a tear when they buried him." Maude looked down at shaking hands that she'd clenched so tightly the knuckles turned white.

Looking back up she continued, "Now, we didn't have the courage to fight back or even run away, but this girl has. I may not know everything she's running from, but I know what it's like to be beat on. So, no matter how old or young she turns out to be, or who she's trying to get away from, I'm going to help her… whether you like it or not."

Maude turned to light the stove, all the while grumbling, "Reckon that's why I never got married, don't have to worry about some man beating on me. And I sure don't have to ask anyone's permission to *do* what *I feel is right*." She punctuated this last statement with an impatient huff accompanied by an indignant glance at Doc.

Doc watched his old friend with a new respect. He'd always figured that Maude's life had been difficult, but he never knew how difficult until today. He could see why she felt such an affinity for their patient, but he was afraid her troubles were going to make Maude suffer all over again.

Shaking his head worriedly he finally spoke, "I can see there's no talking you out of this, at least not right now, but I'm going to think on it tonight and we'll be talking some more tomorrow." He gave Maude a pointed stare emphasizing the meaning of this statement.

"Besides," he teased intending to lighten the awkwardness that had sprung up between them, "I better get. It's about time for me to pass Harriet's house on my way home. She'll be hanging off the front porch, straining eyes, and ears to catch me coming in. On second thought," he stopped, snapping his fingers, his expression animated in mischief, "maybe I'll stay for a while just to see if she'll come check on us. We could sit on the front porch and act like we're sparking," he paused to wink at Maude encouragingly, "drive her into one of those rages again," he chuckled.

"George Carter you won't do! You've been nothing but trouble since you were a boy, I don't know why I put up with you." Maude couldn't help but laugh as she ushered him to the door.

"Now, you be sure and wave real big to Harriet when you pass by, oh… by the way, did you know she thinks you're absolutely amazing?"

"I am," a grinning Doc agreed shamelessly, clambering up in his buggy.

He picked up the reins once more serious and fixed a hard stare in Maude's direction before commanding her to lock and bar the doors.

"You still got your shotguns?" he asked.

Maude nodded as he went on instructing her to make sure they were loaded with extra shells ready at hand. Finally, he slapped the reins gently on the horses to urge them home.

"May as well get ready for some restless nights," he muttered to his horse, "'cause there'll be no sleep till I figure a way to get Maude out of this situation."

Chapter Six

April 17, 1866

Doc Carter drove his buggy doggedly toward town after a six-day stint of doctoring between the Wallace, Alden, and the DuBarry homesteads. All three households were quarantined with scarlet fever; lucky for him they all lived in the same area of the county. He shook his head, saddened by the loss of little Sally Alden, but relieved to get away without losing anyone else. It had been touch-and-go there for a while, but now the children were on the mend.

It felt good to be headed home and he fervently hoped there weren't any emergencies waiting for him; at least nothing that would demand immediate attention. There was mail to pick up at the Mercantile and records to work on later. He was also anxious about the situation he'd left Maude in.

Exhaling wearily, he faced the truth that caring for this whole county was getting to be too much and he was ready for a change. Things had been less demanding in his younger days when the county was sparsely populated, but since the war ended, northerners had bought land on the cheap and moved in to raise big families.

Doc looked back at the time he'd spent treating patients here; on call at all hours of the day or night, rain or shine, cold or hot. When he added the three nightmarish years serving the Confederate Army… well, it had all taken its toll, and he was ready to slow down. He'd recently invited a fresh-faced physician, looking to open or share a practice in this area, to come for a visit. Perhaps if this young whippersnapper was interested, he'd just sell the entire practice.

"Dag blast it! I'm tired; I'd like to do something besides be at everyone else's beck and call, I'll do it," he exclaimed loudly; causing his usually placid horse to break out in a rapid trot.

"Whoa, whoa Jack! You old scaredy cuss… slow down here, for you get us both killed!" he yelled.

Finally getting the horse to settle down, Doc returned to his musings. He'd been reading about the Southwest; its warm climate and breathtaking vistas. He had a hankering to see it, maybe settle there. There'd be fewer people in need of doctoring and surely a body could find a fishing hole somewhere.

"I'm 52 years old and have never been anywhere except back east for college, medical seminars, and the war," he sighed ruefully.

The way he figured it; an extended, maybe even permanent vacation, was long overdue. Perhaps he could convince a certain best friend to come along.

"Dag nab it, that's it; the perfect solution to get Maude away from this situation."

Relieved the decision was settled, he became anxious to get things started and decided to send a telegram to his young doctor friend right away.

"I'm going to ask him to come immediately," he muttered pulling up in front of Harold McNight's Mercantile.

Entering the store, Doc listened to his stomach rumble noisily. He was hungry, tired, and in no mood for conversation. Too late he realized he'd stepped into the wrong place as the door shut and the gaggle of women that clustered around the counter turned to look at him. To make matters worse, Harriet Collier stood right in the middle of them. Simpering sickeningly sweet, she advanced on Doc, hooking her arm through his to drag him over to stand in the midst of the women.

"Here he is ladies the angel that delivered Lenora's baby girl and saved Lenora from the jaws of death," she declared dramatically exaggerating her Georgia drawl.

"Isn't he amazing?" she continued, batting her eyes adoringly up at him.

"My gosh, Harriet, what are you going on about? Give me my arm," Doc ordered severely, jerking his arm free, "I don't have time for this nonsense I got to get out to…"

Here, he broke off abruptly, but immediately wished he hadn't. He could tell by the spite filled look on Harriet's face what she thought his next words were going to be.

"Going to see Maude Sharp again?" she asked too loudly. "How's that redheaded strange man she's keeping in her backroom?" she asked in feigned innocence.

Doc heard the ladies gasp at this revelation and watched the vindictive little gossip as she turned to address the group.

"She told me he was her nephew, but Olivia said Maude didn't have any brothers and sisters. So, we know it couldn't be a nephew," she heralded triumphantly.

Swiping an imaginary speck of dust off the counter she went on nonchalantly, "I went out there to pay a neighborly call the other day, but no one would answer the door. Now, I know she was home 'cause the buckboard was in the barn… I wonder what was going on, hmm…" She let the rest of the statement trail off suggestively.

Doc watched the women titter and whisper among themselves before picking up the package the proprietor handed over to him, along with a look that said, "I share your misery."

Turning to leave, he heard the women make plans to visit Maude and remind her that single upstanding Christian women didn't keep strange men in their homes without a proper chaperone.

Reversing direction, he exploded, sending each woman a hard eyed glare, "I'm going to talk to your husbands. Because apparently, they aren't keeping you busy enough to stop you from sticking your nose in everybody else's business. GO HOME!" he boomed, "tend to your young'uns and quit letting the likes of Harriet Collier get you into situations where you have no business!" He scorched a blazing glower of rage at each woman as he continued.

"You ever wonder why she doesn't have a husband?" he thundered pointing at Harriet, "well keep following around after her and you'll find out. No man wants to be around a nosy spite filled woman bent on causing trouble."

Having said this, he stormed out the door leaving a stunned silence in his wake. Settling quickly on the carriage seat, Doc got his anger in check and picked up the reins. He'd intended to go home for now and visit Maude in the morning, but after hearing Harriet and realizing everyone knew about their patient, he figured they better talk straightway.

"GEDDY UP!" he hollered snapping the reins above the horse, "We have to find out who this girl is and what kind of trouble she could be running from," he muttered.

* * *

Harriet's temper was boiling by the time she entered her little house on the main thoroughfare through Jasmine. Jerking the front door open, she shut it with such force the entire structure shook; causing a crack to fissure across the door's glass pane. Pictures bounced against the wall, with a couple falling to the floor. Yanking the green feathered bonnet off her head, she threw it across the room screeching her vexation.

"Just who does this little country doctor think he is?" she seethed. "Trying to shame me in front of everyone... insinuating men don't want to be around me. Me? The toast of Atlanta society. I'll have him know I had more beaus clambering after my hand than any of these bumpkins here in Jasmine ever dreamed of, especially that Maude Sharp," she spat hatefully.

Walking over to the mirror she preened conceitedly, patting her auburn hair in place while frowning sourly at the faint lines beginning to form around her mouth.

"At least I don't have gray hair like Maude," she placated.

Standing back she surveyed her still trim form critically, "Now, just what does he see in that old cow?" she wondered aloud, skimming her hands over her petite form sensually.

She crossed the room to pick up the fallen pictures trying to calm the agitated fluttering of her nerves. Now wasn't the time to lapse into apoplexy, she had to come up with a way to marry that doctor. The funds from her last marriage were getting low and there was no other means of support. Going home wasn't an option, not after what she'd done. None of her relatives would stand up for her, not even Uncle Barclay and she'd always been his favorite.

"Shoot! I've just got to marry Doc Carter," she exclaimed desperately.

Pacing anxiously, she conducted a mental checklist of all the available men in Jasmine. The judge was married, as was the bank president, and all the other men in town were nothing but two-bit hayseeds with big dreams, limited funds, and tight purse strings. They just as soon see a woman in flour sack rags as pay for the latest Paris fashions.

No, it had to be Doc. He was the one and only choice. After all, they had so much in common; wealthy families, education and a sophistication severely lacking in any other man Jasmine had to offer. Anyway, he should have lots of money stashed away somewhere, being single all these years. Just think, she'd be a doctor's wife, which meant not only financial stability, but reputation and prestige as well.

"Maude Sharp you better stay out of my way because I'm going to marry George Carter by hook or crook," she warned hostilely.

Harriet flounced down on the front window seat staring morosely at the dusty road that provided Jasmine's main thoroughfare of travel. It wasn't much of a town, compared to Atlanta, she surmised. No cobbled streets, no opera house, no dress shops. It was definitely one of the dullest places she'd ever been, even the gossip was boring. But at least no one from home was likely to locate her whereabouts here.

Recalling the journey from Atlanta to Virginia and all the other stops, she hoped the maneuvers and detours she'd taken to cover her tracks would be enough to keep Albert's family from locating her. They'd probably searched from Atlanta to Texas before giving up. Thank God the war had occurred. It gave them a lot more to be bothered about than one chattel they couldn't control.

Maintaining her usual vigil for this time of day, she noticed no lights in any of Doc Carter's office windows, which indicated he wasn't at home. She swore beneath her breath.

"Probably hightailed it out to Maude's soon as he left the mercantile," she muttered angrily.

Leaning forward to get a wider perspective of the road, she gasped excitedly as two unfamiliar horsemen rode into town. They didn't appear to be in a hurry; walking their horses slowly to pull up in front of the Sheriff's office. They were definitely strangers she decided.

"*Now I wonder,*" she questioned thoughtfully, waiting for them to come out.

Harriet watched them emerge, and then amble from the livery to the taverns, the Mercantile, Parkers Boardinghouse, and finally Annie's Home Cooking Restaurant. When the two didn't immediately come out she could stand it no longer. Grabbing her bonnet and reticule, she sashayed out the front door. She'd splurge and have supper at Annie's tonight.

* * *

Hannah awoke feeling well rested and stronger than she had in a long time. It was now several days since she'd awakened from the fever and insensible state that had left a consuming tiredness in its wake. However, bed rest, nourishing meals, and plenty of tender care had set her quickly on the mend.

Glancing around the room, she observed its old-faded wallpaper, sparse furnishings, and the pegs on the wall, from which to hang clothing. Despite this, it was clean and comfortable. Definitely the most pleasant room she'd been in since leaving home, which didn't refer to the rundown hovel she'd been kept in for the past four years.

"*What would it be like to live like this all the time?*" Hannah wondered, but then quickly discarded such thoughts. There were more pressing matters to think about. The best she could figure, it had been at least two weeks since leaving Traders Bluff and Hiram was sure to show up here soon. Reaching for a glass of water on the table, she noticed a large well used book beside it.

"Holy Bible," she read lifting its cover tenderly, letting the pages flutter lightly through her fingers.

This lady sure was a believer in the man upstairs, Hannah thought; recalling the night she'd woke up and listened as Maude prayed for her recovery. That prayer sounded more like she was talking to God… like he was right in the room as she reasoned and made her request. It sounded nothing like the practiced recitals the congregation performed every Sunday in the church back in Oxford.

Shaking her head thoughtfully, she pushed the Bible away as it suddenly reminded her of the one that sat on her poppa's desk. This memory triggered an overwhelming sense of loneliness and homesickness that would have her bawling like a baby if she gave in. Hannah dashed these thoughts. There wasn't time for crying now. She had to get well and get away before the gang came here. Maude really would need God in the room with her if that happened.

Disgusted with her weakness, Hannah decided it was time to get out of bed. She took a deep breath, resting momentarily, before slowly sitting up. The room shifted a little, but quickly settled down and after a brief pause, she lowered shaky legs, placing her feet on the floor.

"So far, so good," she muttered, balancing cautiously on the bedside.

The dizziness returned, but she rose gradually anyway, waiting for the undulating waves to cease, before taking a first tentative, then more self-assured step. Feeling relatively steady, she decided to surprise her caretaker by appearing in the kitchen for supper. Looking around carefully, she didn't see any kind of wrapper to cover her night clothes with. So, noticing how the voluminous gown provided decent covering, she shrugged indifferently and decided it would be enough for just womenfolk.

At last propelled by a fierce determination and slightly shaky legs, she headed toward the kitchen. Rounding the corner, Hannah was brought up short by the sight of Doc Carter sitting with Maude at the table. She hesitated, torn between returning to the safety of the bedroom or finding a chair for her now quaking body. She shook her head, trying to clear the light headedness that was again making things waiver and grabbed the doorframe for something secure to hold onto.

"Come on, missy," Doc called, "do you good to join the living. Besides, we need to talk. Things have changed… it appears the whole town knows you're here now." He paused to watch the effect this information had on the young woman, "Shakes you up a mite, huh?" he asked noting the color drain from an already pale face.

Hannah sank wearily in the chair Maude pulled out and covered her face with trembling hands. She sighed in resignation… that took care of slipping in and out of town quietly. All the gang would have to do is ask anyone and they'd direct them to this nice lady's house.

Lifting her head, Hannah looked at Maude apologetically, "I'm sorry; I never meant to involve anyone else in this. I… just couldn't live like that any longer. Hiram, my… my stepfather is a cruel man and the gang he's in charge of is horrible. I know they'll be coming after me… I'd planned to get out of here without anyone, except you of course, seeing me…" she broke off speaking, realizing the danger her presence placed these people in.

The kitchen was deathly quiet as the seriousness of the situation settled over its occupants. Doc was first to speak, and his tone brooked no argument.

"I know you're determined to get away, but given your condition… well, you're not in any shape to travel, especially by yourself.

Now, my friend here," he continued casting an impatient glance at Maude, "is insisting on helping you, which means I'm roped in on this thing too, since I'm responsible for you being here. So, you're going to have to tell us or the Sheriff or both what you're running from," he finished rubbing his eyes wearily. "On second thought, wait a minute. Maudie you got any coffee on the stove? Heaven knows I could use a whole pot about now."

The room was again quiet, except for the rattling dishes as Maude placed cups of coffee and a plate of molasses cookies on the table. She took Hannah's and added liberal amounts of cream and sugar before teasing kindly, "we need to do all we can to fatten you up, girl. You're nothing but skin and bones."

Ignoring Doc Carter's snort, she continued her efforts to treat their patient gently. A kind word would coax a lot more information from this girl than the brusque demanding tone Doc had adopted ever since bringing her here. Hannah reached for the cup wondering what or how much of her story to tell. On one hand, could she trust them? It had been a long, long time since there'd been anyone to confide in; even her mother had never, as the gang said *"had her back"*. Would they even believe her? Besides, which one of them told everyone she was here?

Replacing the cup back quickly, Hannah stared at both people accusingly, "Why did you have to tell anyone I'm here?" she asked swallowing her anger with a drink of coffee only to choke and sputter noisily.

Doc interrupted immediately, not waiting for Hannah's strangled cough to subside.

"Hold on there," he demanded. "We," he emphasized, "didn't tell anyone. The town gossip called on Maude the other day while you were thrashing and moaning loud enough for the cows in the barn to hear and she came in to look you over. Now, she's blabbed it all over Jasmine that Maude has a tall skinny redheaded man laid up in her bed. How do you think that looks, with her being a single woman and living out here all by herself?" He paused momentarily to calm down.

Maude slapped her hands to her cheeks in mock dismay, "Land sakes George," she exclaimed with twinkling eyes, "the self-righteous brigade will be out here preaching me a sermon. First according to Harriet, the town gossip," she sent an informing glance at Hannah then continued, "insists I'm sparking Doc and now I've got some other man out here." Maude rocked back and forth in her chair laughing gleefully. "I say now, for an old country maid, I'm living a pretty exciting life. No wonder Harriet's so jealous."

Doc jumped up from his chair, forgetting the weariness that assailed him earlier and began pacing anxiously across the kitchen.

He stopped and fixed Maude with a furious look, "I'm glad you can laugh at this, because it makes me madder than fire," he burst out. "And that's just what they aimed to do, before I set them straight… and that blasted Harriet Collier will still probably traipse out here poking her nose around!"

Here, he paused and looked at Hannah, who had sat quietly taking in everything.

"See young woman, they don't even know who you are and you're causing trouble for Maude. What are they going to say when a bunch of outlaws show up because of this person staying at her house?"

"Stop right there, George Carter," Maude cut in sternly, "You brought her here for me to care for, so stop acting like this poor girl came begging to my doorstep." She paused but continued in the same stern tone, "Now, I've never depended on you or anyone else to run interference for me. I've been taking care of myself for the past forty-five years and I've dealt with some pretty questionable characters living this far out. And I can sure take care of the likes of Harriet Collier and Jasmine's fine upstanding ladies"

Mellowing her voice, she continued, "George, my soul is saved… I know I'm fixed with the Man upstairs, so I'm not worried about what happens to me. I've lived my whole life helping others and I'm not about to stop now, so you may as well calm down and choose to help or not, but if you're not… you may as well go home because me and this girl have some talking to do," she finished turning to face Hannah.

Doc huffed and paced, then resumed his seat to gulp down a quick swallow of coffee.

"I'm sorry Maudie," he apologized ducking his head. "I just care about you… I always have… as much as you'd let me." This admission was no sooner out of his mouth before he looked up to declare blazingly, "It burnt me up to hear those biddies going on so… I know enough secrets on every woman in that bunch to send them running out of town, especially that Harriet Collier. I felt like throttling that woman, still may… makes me so mad I could spit nails," he declared glaring at Hannah.

"Well, no need to look at her like that, she's done nothing," Maude interrupted his tirade.

Rubbing his face wearily, he gave Maude a sideways glance before continuing somewhat calmer. "I don't know if I can, I'm mad at everybody; at her, because she's in this mess, at myself cause I brought her here, and you," he glowered stabbing a finger at Maude, "cause you're so durned stubborn about helping her."

He appeared to run out of steam after this, but still managed to vow quietly, "I… I couldn't live with myself if something happened to you Maudie," he stated solemnly, "especially if I brought that trouble to your door."

Maude's cheeks colored prettily following these revelations. This time it was she who reached over to pat Doc's hand tenderly.

"It'll be okay George," she reassured him softly.

Hannah quietly watched their exchange. It was obvious they cared for each other, which put her in a quandary as to how to proceed. Knowing Cutler and Hiram, they'd have no trouble figuring out the tall redheaded man could be her, and as soon as someone gave them directions they'd be out here. And whether she was here or not they'd destroy these two people who'd only wanted to help a pitiful stranger.

Scowling at this self-description, Hannah knew she had to find a way to convince Maude and the doctor to leave Jasmine for good. She recalled overhearing how Cutler had bound and tortured a couple with a hot poker to get information he wanted. Then he just shot them. Hannah shuddered at the thought of these two suffering like that, because of her.

She looked up, noticing that Doc watched her with a questioning stare. She now understood his anger and it dispelled most of her earlier trepidations about his nature. He actually was a kind man and cared as much for Maude as her own poppa had for her mother. Anyone who cared that deeply for another person couldn't be bad. Deciding it was time to trust someone; Hannah took a sip of coffee and started to talk.

"My name is Hannah Elise Todd and I'm 17 years old, but I'll be 18 May 1st, which is why I haven't gone to a sheriff. He'd probably just hand me back over to Hiram and my future would be far worse than the past ever was."

Following this Hannah told them about growing up at the LeClair plantation in Oxford. A stately plantation comprised of around five thousand acres.

"We raised hemp, cotton, hay, and paddocks of pastureland to help support our stable of thoroughbred horses. We also had the only cotton gin in Lafayette County. Our house was beautiful with large rooms well lit by crystal chandeliers that blazed at Christmas with it seemed like hundreds of red candles."

Maude watched the young woman's face come alive in vivid memory of her childhood home for the first time in their brief acquaintance as Hannah continued.

"Grand-mere's hand-painted china, gleaming silver services… Aubusson carpets that stretched from room to hall and right up the double staircases that led to the second and third floor." Hannah looked up grinning mischievously at no one in particular, "I can't count the number of times I got in trouble for sliding down that banister… sure was fun. Nanny would scold me and remind me that all my ancestors were frowning down their lofty noses at my un-ladylike behavior from their portraits that ran along the upstairs gallery."

Doc interrupted brusquely, quickly dispelling Hannah's smiling revelry into the past.

"I suppose you're too young to know how your family came into all this property and wealth… humph," he challenged.

"According to my mother," the undaunted girl challenged back. "Our family has been in the southern part of America since Robert LaSalle reached the Gulf of Mexico and proclaimed it Louisiana for Louis XIV in 1682. This property has been in the LeClair family since 1820 when my great grandfather, a fur trapper and settler Emiel LeClair, rescued a Chickasaw Indian child and the tribe rewarded him with a valley of land in which to settle. Years later, his friendship with these Indians brought about another reward of land when he helped John Martin, John Chisholm, and John Craig purchase land for the actual town site of Oxford in 1837. This reward of tillable acreage was adjacent to what he already owned. So, what had started out as modest beginnings grew to its current vast estate funded by years of successful crops and careful money management."

Hannah had purposefully stared Doc straight in the eye the whole time she'd related this bit of familial history and jerked visibly when Maude interrupted.

"Are there any more relatives… aunts, uncles, cousins… you know the usual kinfolk."

Hannah shook her head negatively confirming her statement. "Unfortunately, my great grandparents Emiel and Louise were the last members of the LeClair family to come to

America and they had only one son whose life ended in a riding accident one week before my mother was born. Stricken by the shock of losing a husband, her mother collapsed, delivered her baby, and died, leaving Irene, my mother an orphan. The will stated that all LeClair assets be deeded to the firstborn of each successive generation, which left my mother very wealthy."

"My great-grandparents raised mother and when great grand-mere died my great grand papa Emiel arranged a marriage between mother who was 16 and, my poppa, James Todd, an older lawyer from Virginia. Grand papa lived long enough to walk mother down the aisle; and then died three months later. My nanny often grumbled about how badly spoiled and coddled mother was. She said Poppa picked up letting mother have and do as she pleased just like great grand papa did." Hannah paused to take a deep breath before continuing, "He was killed during that first battle in Virginia leaving mother even wealthier, but no smarter," she finished wryly.

"Didn't your father have any relatives," Maude asked quietly.

"Papa had one younger brother, Uncle Zachary a physician in Charleston. He came to Papa's funeral and didn't seem to like mother, but she shamed him into staying around to help care for his brother's poor widow, her words not mine, till she could make arrangements for the family solicitor to take over. Unfortunately for him, she never got around to it and as weeks turned into months an amicable relationship between in-laws turned into a battle of wills as mother insisted on resuming her old spending habits while Uncle Zachary did his best to conserve her Yankee dollars. She bitterly complained about his decisions to anyone who would listen and according to nanny tried everything from her feminine wiles to juvenile temper tantrums to get her way."

"Goodness child, did your nanny tell you all this… you couldn't have been very old…"

"Oh no, I heard all this by tagging along with the servants. There were no other children at home and mother never had time for me unless it was to dress me up in some frilly outfit to, as she put it, promenade through town after all she said we're royal descendants." Hannah looked up scowling at no one in particular, "I always hated those outings."

Doc Carter broke into question, "Well then, how did her royal highness get hooked up with the likes of an outlaw like this Hiram Walters you talk about?"

Hannah picked up her family history without challenge to doc's tone. "Apparently, Uncle Zachary had to amputate Hiram's leg from the knee down and he needed a place to recuperate and practice walking. He told mother that Hiram was some big war hero that had been wounded in the same battle as her husband. Playing on mother's vanity he made it look like she would be this man's merciful angel if she'd allow him to stay and perhaps try to cheer him up."

Hannah looked up and chuckled, "Frankly, I think he just was looking for anything to occupy mother's time and get her away from him… Anyway… Hiram and his disgusting cohort Cutler came to live with us. I couldn't stand neither one of them. Nanny kept me as far away as possible from both of them. She insisted there was something evil about these two no accounts, but mother wouldn't listen. Oh, Hiram laid it on thick, pretending all these smooth manners and chivalrous attitudes about helpless women and how they needed to be pampered and protected. I reckon he played mother like a violin, especially after she'd pout and complain about Uncle Zachary's tight hold on the purse strings. Recognizing an opportunity, Hiram began a tentative courtship, pouring on all the courtly gestures and promises of indulgences." Hannah sighed heavily, "And selfish, gullible mother fell for it as nanny said hook line and sinker!"

"Uncle Zachary was ordered to report for duty in Kentucky right after the beginning of January '62. Not one to let an opportunity slip by unclaimed, Hiram proposed to mother, justifying this quick action as a necessity since she'd need someone to care for her and little Hannah and take care of the place. They wed the day before my uncle left."

"Hiram took over, he and mother spent money like water flowing over a dam. They took trips and gave a huge party at LeClair for all the state dignitaries. Nanny said Hiram was taking money and sending it to some address in Traders Bluff, Mississippi. He gambled incessantly and had to pay hush money to several people in town because Cutler had accosted several women. My mother's servant said Cutler was also after the plantation's womenfolk."

"Hiram's lack of experience in managing an estate became obvious that spring. He fired the overseer for questioning his intelligence, which resulted in a hap-hazard planting of the crops. Then he refused to provide funding to repair the cotton gin since others in the county also used it; never mind the fact they paid LeClair Plantation for this service. He insisted they be responsible for its overhaul."

"Once Lincoln emancipated the slaves many of ours ran off and Hiram refused to pay any of them to stay and work. Because of such mismanagement and lack of oversight, along with his and mother's continued spending on everything from gambling, to fashionable clothing, to racehorses, the reality of LeClair's continued existence came crashing down in June of that year."

"The taxes came due, and the plantation was three years in arrears. Apparently, Poppa had either neglected or chosen to not pay the taxes thinking there would be a new Confederate government that would need the money after the war. Unfortunately for

Hiram, the government wasn't letting them slide this time. A desperate examination of the ledgers showed there wasn't even enough money to pay for one year, much less three. The once sizable LeClair Todd fortune was almost gone… run through… six months into the marriage."

"A couple of days later, talk about Cutler's un-chivalrous behavior was rumbling once again. He came to Hiram with an ultimatum to either leave with him or stay and face the situation alone, which meant dealing with debt collectors and his leftover crimes. So, plans were made."

"One night, Hiram divested the safe of all cash and had a servant collect every piece of silver in the house and load it in the buckboard waiting in the carriage house. He informed mother of the situation with instructions to either pack and go with them or stay and face a life of humiliation and poverty."

"Given little choice, mother selected the items she'd take… there was no way she'd stay and face pitying stares from families she had looked down on all her life. Two hours later, around midnight, she lay down with me on a mattress in the back of the buckboard, along with clothing and goods we had been allowed to take." Hannah looked up with tears in her eyes, "I didn't even get to say goodbye to my beloved nanny."

"Finally, after two days of steady travel we reached that secluded ugly cabin in Traders

Bluff, complete with the welcoming team of Elam and Ellis. And while the gang regrouped and was soon up to their old antics, mother and I were introduced to the harsh realities of life without servants and wealth to cushion it. I had just turned thirteen when we went there, and mother died a year or so later."

Doc and Maude listened silently as Hannah described a life devoid of love and kindness or the proper upbringing for a young girl. When she revealed how and why all the scars were on her back, Maude slapped the table as a blazing rage prompted words she never dared to utter before bursting out.

"Why didn't you just shoot him... Oh," she gasped, "what am I saying?" She wrung her hands in frustration, "Why didn't you leave before now?"

Hannah shook her head in resignation, "I tried on my 16th birthday, but Cutler caught me."

She didn't bother to disclose the rest of what he had done before dragging her back.

"This is the first time I've been away from that hovel since the night we left Oxford, except to hunt and fish in the woods."

"How did you get away this time?" Maude asked.

Remembering the events of the morning she left, Hannah described how Hiram woke her up with his whip.

"It wasn't even daylight... so it wasn't like I was lazing in bed," she explained before resuming the rest of the story. Pausing reflectively, she continued, "I reckon I just snapped when he tried to beat me again… He was alive when I left… out cold, but alive. I had to get out while the gang was away."

Sending her companions a determined stare Hannah declared vehemently, "I won't go back there, and I will shoot any of them who come after me."

"Don't you have any kin folks you could go to?" Doc interrupted.

Hannah flinched at his tone, not sure he believed her. "See here, all I've told you is the truth. You can check the Oxford records for proof of our plantation and my mother's family. You'll also find there are no other relatives. Poppa had one brother and he went off to war. Mother was the last of the LeClair's in this country, well except for me. I guess any other LeClair kin would be in France. That's where mother's people were from."

Hannah stopped talking and made a quick decision she hoped she wouldn't regret.

"Maude," she spoke softly, "if you'll bring that old carpetbag that I brought with me, I can show you some things that will back up what I'm saying."

Exchanging a puzzled glance with Doc, Maude rose to retrieve the bag.

Returning, she placed it on a chair beside Hannah. "I would've washed it, but I didn't feel right going through your things," she announced.

Hannah just nodded her thanks and reached into the satchel. She first took out a colt revolver, causing her companions to instinctively draw back as Doc reacted in outrage.

"Now, see here," he burst out only to stop short as Hannah placed the gun on the table.

"That was my poppa's. Mother somehow got it after he died. I took and hid it once we got to Traders Bluff. I was afraid mother would use it on herself… she became strange and well…" Hannah let the words trail off as she rummaged in the bag; this time producing a photograph. Passing it to Maude, she identified the couple in it as her parents.

"My poppa died somewhere in Virginia, fighting with the south. I still miss him," she smiled sadly.

Maude examined the picture before handing it to Doc. It was clear where this girl got her tall lanky body, along with her red hair and light eyes. Doc grunted dismissively as he quickly scanned it, then began pulling on some papers sticking from beneath the frame. These revealed James Todd's military enlistment, a letter dated 1861 to his darling Irene and little Hannah, along with a Yankee $50 bill.

The letter mentioned various concerns, but the one that caught Doc's attention was a mention of the LeClair plantation and trusting Irene to run it till he could get home. This coupled with the rest of the letter and their patient's resemblance to the man in the photograph finally convinced Doc that Hannah was telling the truth. He looked across the table to apologize but stopped as the next thing to come out of the bag aroused his suspicions all over again.

"Land sakes child," Maude exclaimed, "where on earth did you get something like that?"

They all watched in stunned silence as Hannah laid a handful of sparkling gems on the table and then sat staring as if she'd never seen them before. Maude looked at Doc bewildered that this ragged looking girl would have access to such items.

Hannah shook her head in wonder at the sparkling array, "I've always heard about them, but I've never seen them clearly till now," she said breathlessly.

"What are they, no, no I mean where did you get something like that?" Doc demanded, distrust once again coloring his tone.

"Are they real?" Maude asked wonderingly. "They must be worth a fortune," she said nervously.

"These are what's left of the LeClair jewels that have been in my mother's family since Louie XVI. According to mother, her family shared a close kinship with this man. She said a couple of these pieces were actually rewarded by this King to the firstborn daughter of one of my great, great, greats for his bravery in some war back then. Mother used to go on and on about her royal family. Poppa would just grin and say 'Yes, your Majesty'. Hiram never believed the royalty stuff, but he was determined to get his hands on these," Hannah stated, frowning at her companions.

"Anyway," she finished, "with each generation these have been added to and handed down to every firstborn daughter since way back then."

Doc picked up several pieces examining them carefully.

"This clasp says Estelle LeClair," he read squinting to make out the diminutive words engraved there. "This your grandmother?" he asked watching the light reflect off the diamond and emerald necklace.

"I think she's my great, great grandmother," Hannah replied as she pulled out the remaining bejeweled pieces, placing them on the table.

"My gosh," Doc exclaimed his eyes ready to bug out of his head, "how much more of that stuff you got in there?"

"Not much, just Poppa's pocket watch and mother's wedding set," Hannah said laying an intricately carved watch and fob on the table followed by a sapphire necklace, earbobs and wedding rings.

Maude sat stunned by the site before her. The most jewelry she'd ever seen was her mother's cameo brooch and plain gold wedding band. She was almost mesmerized by the beauty of the shimmering stones amidst their gold settings. Doc on the other hand was now more worried more than ever.

"What a mess?" he stated shaking his head. "This is why those outlaws will be after you, isn't it?" he questioned roughly.

Hannah nodded slowly, "Yes, that and the fact that I can identify them," she hesitated before adding the rest. "Cutler doesn't leave anyone alive that knows the gang's activities and can talk about them."

"So, even if you somehow got word to them where these things could be found," Maude asked indicating the items on the table, "they would still come after you?"

"Yes," Hannah said gravely, "and they'll also kill anyone who helps me."

She suddenly sat at attention, observing her companions curiously, "I hope you're not suggesting I try something like that, because I'm not. These are mine and I intend to use them to provide me a much better future than the past 17 years. I'm the last of the LeClair line here and I don't intend to have anyone to pass these on to, nor do I plan to attend any fancy-dress balls where a person would wear something like this."

"But," Maude began only to be interrupted.

"But nothing," Hannah continued defiantly, "Hiram Walters robbed me of my childhood, my ancestral home and most of all my innocence. I'm ruined! When people learn I've spent the last four years living in a house full of cutthroats… alone… unmarried," she paused before voicing a question that had haunted her repeatedly, "What do you think my chances are of living in a town and having any kind of a decent life?" She waited for either of them to respond, knowing there was no comforting or reassuring answer.

"See," she picked up her argument, "all I can do is go away, where no one knows about the Walters gang, or knows my true name and… and live on my own. These jewels," she picked up a strand of lustrous pearls to let them trickle through her fingers, "will provide the money I need to survive."

"Where are you going? What do you plan to do with yourself?" Maude asked, watching her patient with quiet intensity.

"I don't know," Hannah replied tiredly as she began returning the jewelry to its secret pocket in the satchel, "I figured if I ever got away, I'd sell a few pieces of this stuff for necessary funds, then go west… Hopefully there's somewhere out there the Walters gang hasn't been."

Doc handed over the photograph of Hannah's father, minus the papers he'd read. These, he inadvertently placed in his pocket with the intent of confirming her story.

"Ladies," he rose patting his pockets thoughtfully, "I best be getting home. I won't see you tomorrow since I have business to take care of in Memphis. I should be back in a couple of days. Meanwhile, keep this stuff put away, your guns loaded and… well watch out for strangers. And whatever else you do, don't let Harriet Collier in the house."

He stopped talking to look intently at Hannah, "Young lady, you're in a passel of trouble... really all of us are," he shook his head worriedly.

"I... you... we all have to leave!" Hannah erupted. "The men after me are dangerous... horrible, cruel... they'll kill all of us," she insisted.

Hannah felt sick, closing her eyes against the terrible images of what Hiram and Cutler would do to anyone that stood in the way of their intended goal. Maude looked anxiously at Doc who confirmed what Hannah said.

"She's right," he agreed placing his arm comfortingly around his companion's shoulders, "but this is something that's going to take a few days to work out. We can't just up and run willy-nilly, besides she's still weak as a kitten," he indicated gesturing toward Hannah.

Maude began to object, insisting there was no need to just leave.

"We can alert Captain Higgins and he can place some of those smart aleck blue bellies around," she persisted.

"Naw Maudie," Doc said gently, "we have no choice. Those Yankee boys care nothing about really protecting us; they'll be no help."

"But... but," Maude tried to object again only to be cut off as Doc Carter turned to face her taking both of her hands in his.

"Listen, I'm not trying to tell you what to do," he continued firmly, "I'm trying to save your life… Anyways, we're going on an adventure. I was planning to ask before any of this ever happened," he paused to take a deep breath and then forged ahead.

"I'm retiring and moving west and I'm asking you to go with me, so would you… in fact all of us could go together." He stopped watching to gauge her reaction, then rushed on, "This would be a way to help Hannah," he persisted.

Maude stood still, her face a mirror of surprise and bewilderment.

"I… I… don't rightly know what to say," she stuttered at a total loss for words.

"It's okay, just think about it while I'm gone, cause you're going to have to leave one way or another," Doc finished, turning to head for the door.

"Wait," Hannah called holding her hand out, "we're going to need money to leave with. Perhaps you can find a buyer for these in Memphis?" she stated dropping her mother's wedding set in Doc's hands.

Doc stared down at his handful of glittering jewels, "Are you sure you want to get rid of these?" he questioned.

"Yes," Hannah shook her head emphatically. "It's what I intended to do all along. Hopefully, it'll get us across the river to St. Louis," she stated matter-of-factly.

Maude finally found her voice, "so, what are we going to do? Become wanderers roaming all over the west just to escape danger?" she asked raking both her companions with a look of exasperation.

"Something like that," Doc affirmed heading for the front door.

"Talk to her, Hannah," he ordered letting the words trail behind him.

* * *

Harriet sat in the window seat watching the stars appear as twilight gradually gave way to the encroaching darkness. Most of Jasmine was quiet, shut up for the night, the exceptions being Annie's restaurant, whose lanterns were just then extinguished and the raucous goings on at the taverns down at the other end of the road.

Any other night she'd be fighting the urge to go down there and join the revelry. Oh, how she loved to gamble… at anything cards, dice, roulette; Uncle Barclay had taught her well. But tonight her mind was occupied with the men she'd bumped into at Annie's and their ensuing conversation.

They were looking for a runaway girl; tall, with chopped off short red hair and light blue eyes; wearing men's clothing to try and pass herself off as a boy. She was just 17 and had slipped off from home again. According to these men, this girl was a wild hellion always looking for the boys and a good time. Her ma was dead, and her poor crippled pa was trying his best to raise her right, but he couldn't control her anymore. He'd been wounded badly in the war and had a hard time walking, which is why he hadn't come to fetch her home; instead, he'd sent them, her brother Pinkie and Uncle Elam, in his place.

Harriet sat mulling over their conversation. There was something not right about these two. The one named Elam was trying too hard to be convincing and the other one didn't try at all. In fact, he'd kept his eyes on his plate through the entire conversation; only opening his mouth to shove food in it. He didn't appear to care one way or the other if they ever found her.

Now, Harriet knew all about trying to be something you're not and she knew that neither of them was related to this girl or cared one whit about her.

"Oh well, that's neither here nor there," she shrugged nonchalantly; the promise of $100 for information leading to the girl's whereabouts obliterated any thoughts of considering her side of the story. That amount of money was too much to allow conscience to dictate.

Harriet's thoughts tumbled over relentlessly. She couldn't shake the feeling she'd seen this girl somewhere, but where? Looking back over all the new people that had come to town in the past six months, she could come up with only one. The bank president's snobbish sister had come for Christmas, but she sure hadn't dressed like a boy. Harriet fumed, recalling the woman's fashionable clothing. Even now, she still felt drab thinking about her own outdated wardrobe.

"Humph, it's easy to have dresses like that when one didn't have to watch every penny that they spend," she grumbled tonight's supper splurge coming to mind.

And seemingly all for naught! No girls, for that matter or new people, had shown up in Jasmine since last spring. Harriet turned from the window figuring she had as much chance of getting that money as she did of finding a pot of gold at the end of a rainbow. The least those men could've done was pay for her supper, but no… they never even offered.

Hearing a noise outside, Harriet turned back and watched a light appear in Doc Carter's office window.

"I ought to march right over there and tell him how hurt I was by his words this afternoon," she pouted, but then quickly changed her mind.

No doubt he'd been out to that Sharp woman's house all this time… probably still full up of righteous indignation that someone might besmirch his angel's reputation.

"Ooh," she stomped her foot angrily, "makes me sick. I don't have to ruin her reputation; she's done that herself by keeping that man in her bed."

Harriet began laughing at this but stopped abruptly. Wait… that man at Maude's had chopped off short red hair… it had been sticking out everywhere – she remembered excitedly. He had a long body, too. Thinking back, she remembered marveling at such a smooth porcelain face and pretty-shaped mouth on a man. The eyes had been closed, but long dark brown lashes rested on firm young cheeks.

"Jackpot," Harriet cried jumping up, clapping her hands gleefully. "Maude's patient wasn't a man at all. It's that runaway girl and she's going to bring a $100 boon to my finances."

Looking at the clock, she saw it was too late for ladies to be out alone, unless it was an urgent matter. But then, this was urgent. Those men said they would leave in the morning unless something turned up. Pacing impatiently, Harriet debated what to do. She was sure that girl at Maude's was the runaway these men were after, but her conscience was trying to post some objections.

"No, no," Harriet quieted these thoughts while reaching for her black shawl.

That girl's place is at home taking care of her crippled father. Besides, a female that young shouldn't be chasing boys and a good time… one can get in all kinds of trouble doing that.

"I ought to know," she snapped to her reflection in the mirror.

Satisfied that her body was concealed in the voluminous folds of the shawl, she pulled it down over her forehead allowing only the eyes to remain visible. Taking the lamp, she lowered its flame and carried it to the kitchen, placing it on the table. It would be handy for when she returned.

Next, she retrieved a pearl handed revolver and slipped it into her dress pocket. A lady couldn't be too careful alone outside at this time of night. It wasn't that she was scared; she just had sense enough to protect herself rather than give way to fits of screaming and swooning. Patting the gun reassuringly, she let herself out the back door.

Harriet stood for a moment, letting her eyes adjust to the dark before setting off. She chose to go the back way to prevent running in to someone who might question her being out at this hour. Walking slowly and carefully, she kept an eye out for animals, overturned washtubs, or other such implements that could set up a racket if tripped over. That would be sure to bring curious eyes to darkened windows.

She stopped dead in her tracks as Joe Harper's old yeller dog stood and stretched lazily, before ambling around to the front of the building unconcerned. Harriet let out the breath she was holding and hurried on. Finally, the livery came into view. She stood in the shadows watching to make sure no one else was stirring about; like the Sheriff making one of his nightly rounds. Seeing nothing, she darted for the door and slipped noiselessly inside.

It suddenly dawned on her that other men may have decided to bunk here tonight also. Surely, they could find better places to sleep, she surmised, wrinkling her nose in distaste. There was no place in the world that smelled as bad as a barn full of horses. Picking her way carefully down the buildings wide aisle, she looked closely into stalls and wagon beds trying her best to make out two sleeping figures in the dark.

Seeing nothing she whispered loudly, "Mr. Elam are you in here?" receiving no immediate answer she continued, "it's Harriet, the lady you had supper with," she paused again.

"Go on," a voice called out of the dark back stall.

Just then Harriet bumped into a lantern that must've been hanging up high as it banged against her head. Taking it down, she lit a low flame and carried it with her to where the voice came from. Peering over the stall, she saw the two men she had talked with earlier rolled up in their blankets. The younger man acted the same as he had supper, unresponsive and uninterested. The other one sat up flicking straw out of his hair and collar.

"What can I do for you ma'am?" he asked curiously. "It's late and you don't strike me as the type to take a tumble in the hay with a stranger," he smirked.

Harriet drew herself up imperiously and spat, "Well, I came here with information about that girl, but if you're going to talk all vulgar and disrespectful, I'll just go back home and keep it to myself."

Having said this she whirled around, almost upsetting the lantern, only to be stopped by the man's next words.

"Wait, I'm sorry," he said grinning. "It's just that… never mind," he broke off.

He scratched his head thoughtfully before posing another question, "Ain't decent women usually locked up tight by this time of night?" He continued to look at her with an impudent expression that made Harriet itch to slap him silly.

"I'll have you know I'm as decent as any woman in this town," Harriet informed him, her nose still haughtily aloft, "I came out here to help you, but if all you're going to do is insult me…"

"Look lady," Elam interrupted gruffly, "either you got some information, or you don't. You about talked my leg off at the supper table without nary a mention of knowin' where our girl is and now you traipse in here actin' all high and mighty, so tell it or don't. It's been a long day and I'm tired." Having said this he leaned back negligently, waiting within an expectant air.

Harriet stared at the man through angry squinted eyes torn between a raging desire to knock his superior attitude to kingdom come or continue what she started and get that money. Allowing good sense to rule, she let several tense seconds pass before drawing in a deep calming breath and unclenching her gritted teeth.

"Is that reward money legitimate?" she asked suspiciously.

"What's legit-mant?" he asked suspiciously.

"It means," Harriet began with a superior air, "is that hundred-dollar reward for real or are you just saying that to get information?"

Elam reached over and slapped Pinky on the shoulder.

"What'd I tell you boy? You dangle money and they'll come runnin,' ever time." He laughed sending Harriet a mocking sneer, "Yeah," he drawled, "it's for real if the information's worth it."

Harriet's smile resembled an evil grimace as she leaned forward to impart quietly, "I know exactly where your girl is and if you're really serious about finding her, come to my house in the morning at seveb sharp. Oh, and come to the back door. I don't want the gossips in this town spreading that I'm entertaining strange men. Now, I'd better go before someone sees me slipping around here this time of night."

She turned to make a hasty exit but was stopped quickly as Elam asked exactly where she lived. Relating this information quickly, Harriet scurried out of the barn leaving a burning lantern.

Elam moved to extinguish the lantern, expelling several choice words, "no need to burn the barn down," he grumbled.

Returning to his bed role, he reached over and punched Pinky, "Hey, are ya sleep… did ya hear all that?"

Pinky rolled over, pulling his blanket up higher and mumbled, "yeah, I heard."

"Don't ya think it's odd that this old bat is the only person we've come across who knows anything? What do ya think we ought to do… I sure wish Ellis was here," Elam finished glancing over at the silent Pinky with a grimace.

Settling back in his bed role, he kept a steady stream of mumbles about a worthless partner and bossy uppity women. Finally, he lay down.

"Guess we'll go to this woman's house in the morning… seven sharp… better get some shut-eye."

Pinky lay awake long after Elam was snoring. He'd begun to think that Hannah had managed to escape since they hadn't yet found her, but tonight this woman's visit cast a damp blanket over the victory he was feeling. As he lay staring in the dark that sense of being hopelessly trapped almost overwhelmed him. Hannah's escape had given him hope, but if she couldn't get away what made him believe he could.

"No, by gosh," he exclaimed sitting up quickly.

He wasn't going to give up. Neither was he going to have any part in taking Hannah back. He remembered Cutler's warning to Elam and figured since he was holding a gun on Ellis that Elam probably would try to shoot him if he didn't help or tried to get away, but his mind was made up. He was tired of living like this. He'd rather die than have either Hannah or himself return to Traders Bluff.

Chapter Seven

Morning dawned, Elam and Pinky sat in the kitchen of a woman named Harriet, trying to swallow the worst coffee either of them had ever had. An equally pitiful plate of biscuits and a jar of blackberry jam had been placed on the table as a semblance of breakfast. Both made a conciliatory effort at eating, but the biscuits could only be chewed after being thoroughly dunked in the nasty coffee.

One thing for sure, this woman wasn't much of a cook. The only thing really palatable on the table was the preserves and Pinky could have taken a spoon and eaten the entire jar. He would have too if Harriet hadn't chosen that moment to enter the room and take a seat at the head of the table.

"Now boys, we can proceed. The biggest threat to our dealings just caught a ride and headed out of town, so I don't foresee any interference," she beamed; having watched

Doc Carter place his satchel on Saul Jenkins freight wagon headed for Memphis.

Looking squarely at Elam, Harriet wasted no time in getting to business.

"Where's your money?" she asked directly. "I want to see all of it before I say one word."

Her eyes darted expectantly from Elam to Pinky and then back to Elam. A clock ticked somewhere in the house infusing the momentary silence with a nervous tension. Finally, Elam reached in his vest and pulled out several gold double eagles and laid them on the table. Harriet's eyes lit up and she eagerly reached to scoop them up, only to have the money immediately snatched back.

"Not so fast lady," Elam bit out. "Ya ain't told us a thing… not even a hint. Now, ya start talkin' and if what ya say's worth it…I might give ya $50 and if ever thing else pans out, we'll see about the rest."

Harriet's eager smile disappeared as she watched the man across the table through narrowed suspicious eyes. However, keeping an eye on the money, she related being at a friend's house and finding a red headed stranger that resembled the girl they described, including her severe illness and unconscious state.

Elam broke in to ask, "How long ago was this?"

"Oh…" Harriet mentally counted, "'bout four or five days ago. Poor thing, she might be dead by now," she finished with an unconcerned shrug.

Pinky glared at the woman, an expression of disgust plainly revealing his feelings about her. She might dress like a lady and act like a lady, but underneath it all she wasn't any better than Hiram or the rest of the gang… selfish, greedy, murdering trash that'd sell their mothers for money.

He stood up quickly, turning his back before he shot his mouth off. He had to be careful now and not mess things up. Elam believed this woman was really up to something, but he wasn't sure what. If there was a chance, she'd lead them to Hannah. These thoughts were abruptly interrupted as Elam rose from the table suggesting with a taunting sneer.

"How about we ride out and pay your friend a little visit… maybe git a look at this redheaded boy… gal?"

Glancing back, Pinky smirked, watching the woman squirm uneasily. She wanted that money, but she didn't want to be fingered as the person responsible for disclosing the stranger's whereabouts.

At last, Harriet relented and suggested they follow her, "at a distance," she reminded them.

"But," she stated adamantly, "we won't go anywhere unless you hand me that first half you owe me."

She stared Elam square in the face, eye to eye never once blinking or breaking contact until he reached down and counted out $50 in gold.

However, his was the final say, "Lady, I'm givin' ya fair warnin', if this is any kind of trick or your information don't pan out, I'll get that money back… if I have to kill you to do it," he growled.

"So, don't think you're gonna double-cross me or lead me on some wild goose chase, cause you ain't dealt with the likes of me or the rest of my kin." His words trailed off as he turned to Pinky, "Get the horses and bring them back here, while she gets her carriage. We're gonna take a little ride."

* * *

Hannah sat in Maude's sunny kitchen pleasantly full after consuming an enormous breakfast. She'd be fat as a pig after many meals like this, she sighed stretching contentedly. The sun was up just enough to pour in the window behind the sink and flood the room with molten gold that spilled over everything it touched, inciting a warm lethargy in the two women as they lingered over morning coffee. Unfortunately, reality intruded when Maude began asking about Hannah's past life and recent escape.

The girl spared no details, hoping to impress upon her companion the kind of men that made up her stepfather's gang. So far, Maude wasn't convinced she should just pick up and leave.

"Why, they have no idea where you are and nobody in town knows who you are, not even Harriet Collier. They just think I have some man stashed out here," she reasoned.

Hannah sighed worriedly.

"How long do you think it'll take them to figure out the tall stranger with red cropped hair at your place is me? Are there any other red-haired people with cropped off hair in Jasmine?" She paused to allow Maude time to mull this over before continuing, "And, how long do you think it will take before they're here, threatening to burn your house down if I don't come out and give up?"

Watching Maude shake her head negatively, Hannah continued, "These men don't just rob people. Oh no! There's one… Cutler, who's got quite a reputation for molesting women. There's an actual wanted poster for him in Arkansas and Texas." She hesitated, weighing her words carefully before revealing in grim detail some of the methods of intimidation and torture the gang used to make people talk.

"And," Hannah expelled the next statement in a deep breath, "they consider anyone that might've seen, heard or helped their victims get away to be enemies and therefore fair game."

Hannah stopped talking, noticing Maude had grown pale. She felt bad about frightening this lady and started to apologize, but was interrupted by her quiet, but furious exclamation, "These… these aren't men… they're nothing but fiendish animals," she finally breathed out.

"Why hasn't the law caught up with them?" she glared angrily at Hannah, before burying her face in her hands.

Several quiet moments passed until Maude controlled her emotions enough to look up and smile shakily.

"I'm sorry; it's not your fault… It's just that I've never faced anything like this," she explained to justify her reaction.

"I know," Hannah responded. "You don't have anything to apologize for. I'm just sorry you got brought into this."

Rising abruptly, she paced to the window announcing vehemently, "I wish Doc had just left me lying in the road and let me die there. At least I'd be free and no one else could get hurt."

"No, no," Maude turned to face Hannah, "you mustn't say things like that. You've done nothing to be ashamed of or apologize for. I'm glad you ran away… glad Doc found you and brought you here. I don't see how you stood it the last four years. It's a wonder you're not touched in the head by now," she broke off with a shuddering breath.

Hannah smiled wryly.

"Believe me, you may think I am before this is over, because from here on out it's their life or ours. I laid awake many nights and heard Cutler laugh about doing the things I told you." She watched Maude's face carefully as she made her next statement, "I don't want to kill anybody, but I will and now you may have to if we're going to live."

Maude inhaled a shaky breath. "I'm not going to kill anyone, Hannah. I may have to wound them severely, but it's not my place to take another's life."

Hannah looked at her companion incredulously, "you wouldn't kill a man to save your life?" she sputtered. "What about doc's life?"

Maude shook her head, answering quietly, "I don't think so, but I guess I'll have to wait till the situation occurs before I can answer that for sure. I'll admit I'm pretty shook up."

She peered at Hannah narrowly, "Are you afraid?"

Hannah smiled sadly, "I've been afraid for the past five years; ever since Hiram walked through the doors of our home in Oxford. Afraid mother would marry Hiram. Afraid he'd kill her after we moved to Traders Bluff and after she died, I feared being killed or molested in my sleep, or whipped to death. Worst of all I was afraid I'd never get away from those brutes. Well, I managed to get away and I'm not going to let fear cheat me of my chance at freedom. So, make no mistake, I'll kill the first one of them that tries to stop me."

"I..." Maude's response was abruptly cut off as both women turned to listen to

Clyde's howl announcing someone approaching the house.

Maude rushed to the parlor window and peaked out. Grimacing distastefully, she ordered Hannah to get her valise and hide.

"It's Harriet Collier! That busybody," Maude huffed impatiently. "She has a sneaky way of somehow getting in your house before you realize what's going on, but I'm determined it's not going to happen today."

Hannah was about to argue, but quickly changed her mind after receiving the fierce scowl directed her way.

"Hurry," Maude demanded, "I'll get rid of her. Just don't show yourself, no matter what you hear. Besides, the shotgun is right by the door all I have to do is reach in and grab it. I may have to fire a shot over the carriage to get her to leave. You know… convince her I mean what I say. Go on," she insisted anxiously.

Hannah moved quickly, stopping long enough to hand Maude the Colt pistol from her bag, "Here, hide this in your skirts. It's fully loaded and cocked so be careful."

She ducked behind the kitchen door, peaking cautiously around to watch Maude step outside and pull the front door partially closed. Then, she hurriedly sped to stand behind the door to listen; ready to intervene if necessary. Maude stepped out, shielding the door with her body, and waited for Harriet to bring the buggy to a halt. She watched the woman with a cold silent stare that clearly stated there was no welcome here.

However, heedless of this ominous sentiment, Harriet called out in a jeering singsong tone, "Mau-de, you've been found ou-out! Guess what Olivia Cole told me."

She waited, but no response came, "Well-ll," she drew the word out dramatically, "said she's known you all her life and that you didn't have any brothers or sisters," she paused tapping her chin seemingly in thought, "but you said that sick boy in your back room was your nephew... imagine that?" she mocked; preparing to alight from the carriage.

"Hold it right there," Maude demanded sternly. "No need to get down Harriet, you won't be staying."

"Well, I never," Harriet squawked in feigned shock, settling back in her seat. However, her umbrage swiftly changed to an expression of self-satisfaction as she delivered her next volley.

"That's okay, I can talk from here. Guess what else I found out..." she waited expectantly.

"What's that?" Maude asked her impatience with this exchange openly obvious.

"It appears that red haired person you're keeping isn't a boy at all." Harriet waited again, enjoying this guessing game.

"He's not," Maude continued playing along.

"No," the woman in the buggy announced smugly. "He's nothing more than a 17-year-old girl that's run away from home and left a poor old, crippled daddy with no one to care for him."

"You don't say. How did you find that out?" Maude challenged.

Harriet leaned over to peer around the carriage, then straightened to face the seemingly unflappable woman on the porch.

"See those two men back there in the trees," she gloated.

Maude glanced in the direction Harriet indicated and inhaled sharply as her hand tightened on the pistol in her pocket. She glanced back at Harriet noting the gossip's smirking expression.

"I see your friends," she replied coolly… "New suitors of yours… or did you bring them for me, perhaps to set me off Doc?"

"No, you ninny," Harriet sputtered plainly annoyed. "They're that girl's kin. Her brother Pinky and Uncle Elam come to take her home."

Maude heard a gasp from behind the door and knew Hannah hadn't done as she was told. Hopefully, that was as far as the girl would come.

Thinking rapidly Maude announced, "Well, I'm sorry you went to so much trouble, but I'm afraid you've brought those men out here for nothing. That boy you saw in my back room high tailed it out of here two days ago, sometime in the middle of the night. Never said goodbye, thank you, or nothing," Maude finished noticing one of the men gradually easing closer to the house.

Harriet stared intently as though carefully weighing the truthfulness of this revelation. Pretending defeat, she sighed regretfully.

"Well, Uncle Elam, I guess we're too late," she announced leaning around to address the man on horseback, causing him to hold up.

"But Maude," she again moved to get down from the carriage, "you may as well be neighborly and invite us in for some refreshment since we've come all this way. Why, I'm just parched."

Maude stood silently, her stoic expression revealing nothing of the tumultuous thoughts incurred by Harriet's self-imposed visit. Knowing she had to act fast or bodily wrestle this woman to keep Hannah safe, she quickly pulled the pistol from her pocket and shattered the grim waiting silence with the loud crack of a gunshot.

Harriet's horse jerked in alarm and lurched in its harness, rocking the carriage precariously and throwing its startled passenger back in her seat.

"Who's firing guns?" she demanded scrambling to retrieve the reins.

Finally, getting the horse under control, she looked up to see a .44 colt revolver pointed straight at her.

"Now," Maude stated in a determined cold tone that dared anyone to challenge, "I've already told you. You won't be staying so I'd remain in the carriage if I was you. And, and you there," she hollered at the men, "I don't know this girl you're looking for. So, I've got nothing else to say to you; Best to be on your way." Maude stood stiffly, trying hard not to let the quaking inside her body transcend outwardly.

"I never," Harriet finally gasped. "I'm going to get the law and tell them you're harboring a young runaway and won't hand her over to her honest kinfolk and that you almost killed me," she shrilled preparing to turn the buggy around. However, Maude's next words brought an immediate cessation of movement.

"I dare you," her nemesis challenged. "You see Harriet, Doc knows all about your dirty secrets and he told them to me."

Maude watched the woman in the buggy visibly shudder and fumble the reins. It didn't deter her.

"What was his name? Albert...? Your supposedly dead husband? His family is looking for you. It seems Doc ran across Robert Cooper in Atlanta at his last medical meeting. Apparently, he's been looking for you ever since the war ended."

Maude breathed a sigh of relief as Harriet picked up the reins, yanked the horse around and headed back toward town like a scalded cat. However, the men hadn't budged. The one closest to the house watched her closely as though debating whether to charge the house or not. Finally, he hollered loudly.

"Hannah, we know you're here and we're gonna leave. See, I know you probably got a gun trained on us right now and we're not fool enough to rush the house…'tween you an' this harridan on the porch… well, me and Pinky are sittin' ducks, but mark these words… we'll be back and bring the rest of our kin along… ya hear?" He waited, not taking his eyes off Maude who still stood unwavering with her pistol trained straight on him.

At last, he wheeled his mount around and galloped down the road calling for his partner to follow.

* * *

Harriet pulled sharply on the horse, bringing the buggy to an abrupt lurching halt in the back of the small house. Her rattled thoughts were obvious as hurried irregular actions caused her to trip alighting from the carriage and stumble gracelessly to the door. Her mind fluctuated between the two dilemmas she now faced; first, she'd been found out, which led to the second, deciding where to run next.

She wouldn't let them take her back to Atlanta. Besides making her the laughingstock of the city, they'd for sure put her in prison. It was a tossup between which of these fates would be worse. Just the thought of public ridicule and self-righteous sneers from Atlanta society was enough to make her nauseous, and the possibility of prison confinement brought on a smothering sensation so strong she had to grasp the doorknob and take several deep breaths to keep from passing out.

Somewhat regaining her composure, she entered the house and began pacing the cluttered, messy kitchen wondering how long-ago Doc Carter had learned her secret. Had he revealed her whereabouts? If so, how close could they be to finding her?

"And just think. Now Maude Sharp knows all about me… of all people, why does it have to be her?" Pausing mid-step, Harriet clenched her fist and muttered with abject abhorrence, "I hate that woman… too bad I don't have time to make her my special stuffed mushrooms."

Grinning maliciously at the thought of her rival retching out her last breath, the distressed woman entered the bedroom and pulled out two large valises, opening them on the bed. Making quick decisions she chose to take only her newest frocks; let the good ladies of Jasmine have the old ones, after all, fashion was wasted on this backwoods village.

Her thoughts raced, evaluating the farthest yet most advantageous locations to settle in, which this time meant heading farther west. Until now, she'd felt safe in the obscurity of this little town. She'd planned to marry

Doc and move him to either Memphis or St. Louis, but of course that was out of the question now, and settling there alone wasn't an option either.

Harriet stopped packing for a moment to consider California, but shook her head, that was a last resort. The city of Denver came to mind.

"That's it," she exclaimed.

Why not head to Denver? There was a lot of talk about gold out there and where there was gold there was sure to be gambling, along with a variety of men. She'd heard women were scarce in the west, so those female-starved boozed-up miners ought to be easy pickings; especially for someone with her skills at cards and Faro. Denver is a long way from Atlanta too, she concluded with a satisfied smile.

The more this idea developed, the more promising it seemed, and she quickly finished packing, cramming clothes and toiletries haphazardly into the bags. The last two items she never traveled without; a. 41 Remington Derringer was loaded and slipped in the pocket of her skirt while a pearl handled switchblade was hastily slid into the sheath inside her high-top button shoe.

Picking up the valises, she headed to the kitchen and retrieved a small leather pouch from a dented peach can hidden behind the cook stove. Emptying its contents, she counted swiftly and accurately, $600 in crisp Yankee money. This was the remainder of what she'd taken from Albert's safe seven years ago.

"Oh well," she sighed taking the money to stand before a large mirror in the front room.

Peering vainly at her reflected image, she folded the bills and shamelessly addressed the woman looking back, "I'll just have to find another fortunate opportunity. Surely somewhere between Memphis and Denver there'll be a lonely rich old man. Men," she sneered, "they're all the same everywhere. Give them a little lovin' and pettin' and let them think you need their protection and they'll be eating right out of your hand."

Having delivered this gem of knowledge, Harriet stuffed the bills down the front of her shirt waist, securing them beneath the top of her corset. She knew better than to keep a large sum of money amongst her belongings. Baggage was the first place robbers searched when holding up travelers.

Tossing the leather pouch carelessly aside, she took a swift survey of each room to make sure there was nothing to verify her occupancy here. However, on second thought she retrieved the leather pouch, recalling how The First Deposit Bank of Atlanta was displayed prominently across the small bag.

"No need to get careless now," she admonished, shoving it in her pocket before making sure the $50 she'd earned this morning was tucked safely in her reticule.

Satisfied, she returned to the kitchen, picked up her valises and proceeded outside to the waiting carriage. Stowing the bags securely behind the seat, she hurriedly watered the horse and climbed aboard the buggy, and after thoughtful consideration, decided to take the road that led to Olivia Cole's house. No one would think twice about seeing her head this way, she often visited the town's second best gossip. But today, instead of taking the turn-off, she'd stay on the main road and continue on to Memphis. There, she'd cross the river and head west. Now, she smiled smugly to come up with a new name.

* * *

Pinky heard Elam's call to leave and with some indecision, turned to follow. He considered refusing to go but couldn't be sure Hannah or that woman on the porch would believe his intentions. From the looks of things, the odds weren't in his favor. Shrugging dejectedly, he set his horse in motion, trailing behind unhurriedly. They'd been on the road a while when Elam abruptly wheeled his mount around glaring irritably.

"Boy, what the Sam Hill is wrong with ya? Lolly-gaggin' back here like we got all the time in the world… we got to git back and let 'em know we found the little wench 'fore she gets too far away. She must feel pretty slick, thinkin' she done give us the slip. Man, I cain't wait till Hiram catches up with her," he snickered.

Pinky said nothing, but urged his mount to catch up, not wanting to rouse any suspicions.

"I'll give you this much," Elam continued, "you're one of the talkin'est partners I've ever rode with. Why a feller could go plumb deaf from all the jaw flappin' you keep up." He sent the boy a sardonic smirk before continuing, "I know Cutler told you to keep your mouth shut, but there ain't nobody to hear now; so, you can at least say somethin' once in a while."

Pinky shook his head and grinned before responding loudly, "Somethin'."

"Hey, hey, ho, ho ain't you the funny one," Elam growled. "I sure wish Ellis was here."

They rode through the afternoon in silence, winding their way along a swift little creek. Around sunset Pinky brought his horse to a stop.

"Let's camp here tonight. There 'pears to be some fish in that water and I'll catch a mess and cook 'em. Besides, we gotta stop somewhere and this looks as good a place as any." He paused, waiting for Elam's lead before dismounting.

Waving a wordless consent, Elam pulled up and began tending the horses, while true to his word, Pinky caught a huge mess of fish. He was in the midst of cooking them when a stranger riding a large dapple-gray gelding hailed the camp.

"Hello, the camp! Mind if I get down and share your fire? Whatever you're roasting there sure smells good."

Noticing the man's clerical collar Pinky immediately assented without bothering to consult Elam. His mama always said, '*Never turn a parson away from your door chances are they're one of God's angels.*'

Elam gave Pinky a warning scowl before turning to face the stranger.

"You're travelin' kind a late in the day ain't ya, I mean for one of your kind."

The man dismounted and approached Elam with an outstretched hand; a friendly smile creased his face.

"You mean my kind is not supposed to travel after dark?" he responded good-naturedly. "Name's Gideon Mason, I was trying to make it to Jasmine before dark, but it looks like that's not going to happen. I'd appreciate your hospitality for tonight. That food smells mighty good," he nodded toward the fire. "I'll be glad to pay, if you have enough."

He waited, understanding that decisions between these two were really up to the guy in front of him. He'd caught the stern scowl directed towards the boy a minute ago.

Elam looked the man up and down taking note of the gun belt he wore.

"I never heard of a parson wearin' a gun," he stated suspiciously.

The stranger grinned affably, "Well, a man never knows what kind of fix he'll find himself in on the trail; no matter if he's a parson or a peddler. Besides, it comes in right handy for shooting your supper, especially if you don't find a friendly fire with someone already cooking, but…" He pulled back the proffered hand and turned to go. "I'm not looking for trouble, so I'll move on down a piece."

Elam continued to look uneasy, but finally relented with a stern warning, "I reckon ya may as well stay seeing as its dark, but none of that sermonizin' ya hear?" Not bothering with introductions, the surly man turned his back and strode away.

Acknowledging Elam's demand with an amenable nod, the parson walked away to settle his horse. Supper was a quiet affair, the silence broken only by the reverend's mumbled blessing over his food along with the sounds of utensils hitting tin plates and coffee slurps.

Gideon got the feeling that something wasn't quite right between these two, but he couldn't put his finger on it. The boy seemed harmless but looked ready to jump right out of his skin. The other man had that guarded, hardened look of someone up to no-good and certainly not one to be trusted. That demand about "no sermonizing" hadn't come as a surprise either.

He'd been told that many times by men such as this one; shifty characters pursuing dishonest activities unwilling to spend time with someone in his line of work. He figured just his appearance symbolized a light that illuminated their evil deeds; made them down-right uncomfortable. Too bad he couldn't be scared off with cold shoulders and indignant annoyed stares.

He'd developed a thick skin a long time ago; learning to fight and survive, first in the orphanage where he grew up, then as a Texas Ranger; a lot of tough years, but that was past. A few years ago, he'd given his life to God, determined to defeat the enemy the best way, *God's way*, pursuing souls that would never find their way inside a church. Releasing a deep tired sigh, he refilled his coffee and retrieved a worn black Bible from his saddle bag.

"Mind if I read the good book before we turn in," he asked settling back by the fire.

Noting the young guy's eager look, he started to read aloud, only to be stopped by the one in charge.

"What did I tell ya parson?" Elam asked directing a steely glare across the fire, "we don't want your religion. Me and the boy got to be up early and head out at first light. Now, if you want to read go ahead, but keep it to yourself," he ordered rudely, tossing a saddle blanket to the boy along with a meaningful stare.

Gideon watched the boy comply without complaint, and then turned to his study.

"Okay Lord," he sighed inwardly, "I know you sent me here, but why if they're not going to listen." He shook his head and began reading.

A few scriptures later, he felt a calming peace along with a compelling urge to be patient. Humbled, Gideon bowed his head, "Yes Lord," he silently acquiesced and continued studying.

Pinky stretched out anxious for the parson to turn in and Elam to start his usual snoring. He was almost too keyed up to lie still as the dream of freedom finally seemed possible. He figured tonight was as good a time as any to slip away, especially with an outsider present. Surely, Elam wouldn't shoot him in front of a stranger, particularly a man of God. He turned slightly, covertly watching the parson's quiet movements.

There was something different about this parson from all the preachers he'd seen in church. This one was dressed in black dungarees and a black fringed buckskin shirt that displayed a wide white collar, resembling the apparel of the minister. His manner was different too, more open, and less judgmental. Also, Elam's frosty treatment didn't seem to bother him. Usually, preachers backed away once the gang talked rough like.

Pinky yawned quietly; deciding it was the gun. He'd never known a preacher that wore a gun belt. He studied the man, wondering about his age with his silver hair, yet unlined face; not that he was any judge of age. Oh well, he exhaled silently, this man sure was odd for a preacher, if he really was a preacher.

It seemed to take forever, but at last the parson turned in and Elam could be heard snoring loud enough to drown out the usual night sounds. Moving stealthily, Pinky rose and stood quietly, looking around to locate at least one of his partner's weapons; not that he had any intention of using it, but it might work as a bluff if Elam pushed things.

Pinky moved, cautiously skirting the fringes of camp, freezing in place at the least movement from either of the men. Stumbling over an unfamiliar object, he realized the parson must have moved his bed roll further from the fire and now lay directly in the shortest, clearest path to Elam's pistol.

However, a careful scrutiny of this arrangement revealed an easier, less threatening access to a weapon. The preacher's gun belt lay totally unguarded, right behind the man's head. Pinky's first thought was how none of the gang would be this reckless... for no one sleeping in the open would leave their pistol so far out of reach; but it sure made things better for him.

Taking a deep quiet breathe, he bent down, gradually eased the pistol from its holster and then straightened upright slowly. Keeping a watchful eye on the sleeping parson, he stuffed the weapon in his waistband and crept carefully toward the horses; silently willing them to not make a sound. A gust of wind blew, rustling the trees overhead, raising goose bumps down his spine and with quaking knees he reached to lift a saddle. Feeling something push firmly into his back, he stiffened immediately, dropping the saddle back in place.

"Thinkin' on leavin'?" Elam demanded in a grating hushed voice.

Pinky swallowed audibly and broke out in a cold sweat. Mustering courage both real and imagined, he pulled out the pistol and quietly cocked it with much trepidation.

"I... I'm through Elam," he stammered. "I... I'm not going back. You can go on, tell 'em where Hannah is, but I'm havin' no part of it."

Gaining confidence, he spun around and spat out, "I'm tired of bein' forced to live and do the things y'all make me do and here's where it ends."

"Where did you get that?" Elam demanded indicating the gun. Glancing around he saw the empty discarded holster and smirked, "I see ya took the parson's pistol... smart move, but... you're not gonna use it. Look at ya," he taunted, "shakin' like a leaf. It's just like Cutler says, too sissified to hold a gun." He paused, watching Pinky closely.

"You know, I'm just gonna have to take it from ya. Cause sure as the sun comes up in the east, you're goin' back to Traders Bluff with me. In fact, since we're up, we might as well saddle up and ride out now. We'll just forget what just happened here if ya come on." Totally confident that Pinky would follow suit, Elam holstered his pistol and turned to saddle a horse.

"No… I ain't goin' nowhere with you," Pinky stated feeling nerves tighten as Elam spun back around and took a step toward him.

"Never again," he continued, "I didn't volunteer to join your gang that day in Fayetteville, Cutler forced me, and he's made it clear that it's either ride with you or die. Well, I've been lookin' for a chance to get away ever since and this is the first one to come along. So, I'm takin' it." He stopped to take a deep shaky breath.

Stepping back slightly, he stared Elam square in the eye, leveled the trembling gun at his middle and rushed on before losing his nerve.

"Now, I'm saddlin' this horse and headin' north. I don't think you want to shoot me in front of a stranger," Pinky said quickly, noticing the parson's rapid arousal from sleeper to watchful observer. "I didn't get this gun to shoot anybody with, but I… I want you to understand… I'm not goin' back."

Pinky glanced nervously to the side, noting the parson's noiseless approach behind Elam. Unfortunately, the savvy outlaw must have detected it too.

"Hold it right there, preacher man." Elam barked out sharply, keeping a cold stare trained on Pinky. "This is between me and the boy."

Taking a wide step forward he thrust out his hand, "Give me the gun," he ordered waiting, "I said, give me that gun, you little worm," Elam ground out through clenched teeth.

"Ain't no snot nosed little boy gonna cause me to lose my brother. 'Member…'member Cutler said he'd kill Ellis if you don't come back dead or alive, well, it's your choice… now, I don't want to put a bullet in you, so quit foolin' around and let go of that pistol!"

The last words were barely out before Elam's hands clamped firmly around Pinky's grip on the gun and he began tugging. They struggled heedlessly, neither listening to the other as Elam attempted to wrestle the gun away and Pinky tried to make clear why they needed to stop pulling.

"No, Elam, don't pull… my finger's around the trigger… you got my hands…"

"You're only making this harder on yourself, now turn…"

Elam's eyes widened alarmingly… Pinky's words faltered… As a gun blast exploded, quelling the struggle while sending recoil spasms to quake up his arm and spread through his entire body. He watched in mute alarm as a small red spot appeared in the middle of Elam's chest, growing larger minute by minute. Gradually, the man's hands, that had been crushing his only seconds before, lessened their grip as his knees buckled and he crumpled slowly to the ground.

Pinky stood silent, motionless, the horror on his face speaking loudly all the disbelief and torment he felt while watching the wounded man moan pitifully in the dirt.

"Oh Pinky... Oh Pinky," he whined. "Ya killed me. I cain't believe ya killed me."

This lament roused the boy and he dropped to his knees beside the writhing partner.

"Elam... Elam, I'm sorry, I'm sorry. I was tryin' to tell ya not to pull," he uttered in despair. "Be still... We'll get some help. Here," he looked around frantically.

"The parson will help. He can ride to Jasmine. I saw a doc's office there... just hold on... we'll get ya fixed up in no time and you'll be right as rain... you'll see." He moved to call the parson but was stopped short as Elam's bloody hand clutched his arm.

"No... no time," he uttered in a shallow breath. "Tell El--tell El," he struggled for a moment before taking a last shuddering breath and suddenly with all the life left in his body yelled loudly, "E-L-L-I-S." He then lay still, staring sightlessly up at the star filled sky.

The sound of that name seemed to hang eerily in the air and Pinky sat unnerved beside the dead outlaw waiting for its resonance to recede. Suddenly, his body began shaking uncontrollably from a combination of nerves and silent wrenching sobs. Elam was gone and he was now responsible for taking another man's life. Burying his face on his knees, Pinky gave way, uncaring of who heard or witnessed his sorrow. A gentle hand touched his shoulder, but provided little consolation; instead, an anguished rumble of fear and self-condemnation poured forth.

"I never meant to shoot. I-I've never shot a gun at anyone," he sobbed. "Wha-what am I gonna do now?" He raised tear filled eyes to the parson. "I-I killed a man, I killed a man," he mumbled over and over disgustedly.

Gideon pulled the forlorn boy to his feet and walked him over to the remains of the evening fire. A cool wind stirred, chilling the air, prompting the parson to feed the embers a few dry leaves and twigs to coax it back to life. Hoping to help the boy get past this initial reaction, he rose and placed his hands on the kid's thin shoulders and gently pushed until he sank down to stare unseeing into the fires dancing flames. A waiting silence settled over the camp with the exception of a few lingering sobs punctuated by deep gulps for air as Pinky tried to rein in his emotions.

"Drink," Gideon commanded, thrusting a cup of lukewarm coffee in the boy's hands.

It was left over from supper and was now strong enough to hop from the cup and walk on its own. Hopefully, that acrid taste would be enough to shock the kid out of his dazed misery. The first drink was swallowed automatically with little notice of taste. However, the second one brought about the desired effect. Pinky shook himself, then frowned sourly at the parson before pitching the thick black liquid in the fire.

Gideon shrugged good-naturedly, "I just wanted to bring you back. It was either that or knock some sense into you. Fortunately, I believe in taking the less violent approach first."

"Yeah, like I should've done," Pinky offered, shaking his head as tears clogged his throat.

"Elam's lying dead over 'cause for once I grabbed a gun. Would you believe, I-I've never aimed a weapon at another person before tonight," he asked, looking at the parson beseechingly.

Gideon cleared his throat thoughtfully before asking, "Why tonight then? What made this one time different?" He watched the boy struggle for a response, leaning back unhurriedly. Finally, the kid started talking.

"I wanted to get away... For the past eight or nine months they've made me do and be part of things that I never, in my wildest dreams, thought I'd be a part of. Things," he shuddered disgustedly, "that I'll never be able to forgive myself for. And now... I've done the one thing I was so determined they'd never make me do." Pinky looked the parson in the eye and muttered with much self-reproach, "I killed a man."

"Yes, but that wasn't your intent, now was it?" the parson asked quietly. "I heard you tell Elam your finger was caught and to not pull on the gun. Did he listen?"

Giving the kid time to think he emptied his canteen in the battered coffeepot, then added fresh grounds. The silence lengthened as Pinky furrowed his brow in recollection of the past hour.

At last Gideon continued, "All your partner had to do was take his hands from the pistol or simply not pull like you told him. So, no kid, you didn't kill anyone. Elam was the one to pull that trigger. The man just killed himself."

"Are you sure?" Pinky asked wanting to believe this man's words.

He watched the parson's face closely looking for any sign of condemnation before continuing, "But, I'm the one who pointed the gun."

Gideon nodded solemnly and made sure he had the kid's eye before going on, "as God is my witness, I promise I'm telling the truth. Furthermore, I don't believe you have it in you to shoot anyone, not even to save your own life."

"That's what Cutler said, among a lot of other things," Pinky mumbled looking down as though embarrassed. "The gang all made fun of me 'cause of that."

Gideon shook his head regrettably over man's cruel nature and pressed the kid for details about his life.

"Tell me about this gang and how you came to be in it," he stated, rising to take a blanket and cover Elam's body.

Pinky began haltingly at first, but with each stuttered word he revealed in detail his capture and the despicable activities he'd been forced to be a part of. The parson listened grimly, realizing this kid had ridden with the infamous Walters gang, whose depraved activities made them a target for sheriffs and bounty hunters alike. It was a desperately shameful and scared boy called Pinky by his captors, who now revealed details that law enforcement across five states and territories had been trying to find out for the past six years. Pinky finished his discourse by relating why he and Elam had been in Jasmine, including Hannah's desperate situation. At last, he stopped talking and stared morosely at the fire.

"I-I guess you'll have to turn me in to the law now," he finally stammered unable to look directly at the parson.

Gideon sat quietly mulling over all he'd just heard before answering the kid's question with one of his own. "Pinky, hmm… Let's end this right now. Do you have a moniker other than Pinky?" He watched the boy's face flush a vivid color reflecting the nature of his nick name and waited for the answer.

"When you decide to reveal that I want you to look me in the eye and answer truthfully this next question." He waited till the boy lifted shame filled eyes to look directly at him before going on. "Did you at any time take part in any of their deeds… hold someone down, enter a bank… exactly what did you do?"

Pinky stared unblinkingly at the parson and answered without waiver or hesitation.

"My real name is Calvin Simmons, and my job was to stay with the horses, make sure they were ready to ride so everyone could get away. I was to watch for the law or anyone that might come by and interfere, but I never went inside a bank or close to a stagecoach or inside anyone's home where the rest of them were busy."

He paused to take a deep breath before continuing, "sometimes, I could see what they did and other times I would hear women scream and Cutler and the rest of them laughin'. I'd get plum sick to my stomach, but I daren't say a word… I was too afraid of what they would do to me," he finished with snort of self-disgust. "Doesn't say a whole lot for me does it?selfdisgust."

Gideon watched the kid hunkered close to the fire, shoulders sagging, head hanging; weighed down by a mantle of self-loathing and defeat. Apparently, he wasn't going to run. He hadn't once attempted to mount up and ride away; hadn't even glanced toward the horses. And his emotional state made it clear that killing another human either accidentally or on purpose just wasn't in his makeup.

Throughout all his years of law service and soldiering, he'd seen the reactions of many young boys who'd taken the life of another human for the first time… victims of circumstance; certainly not hardened killers or criminals like the Walters gang.

So, how to answer the kid's question? He knew the law… knew that any other lawman would most likely hang this boy simply because of who he'd ridden with and bounty hunters. Well, they'd probably put a bullet in his back claiming he tried to escape. It wouldn't matter that he was a victim of this gang, caught in the wrong place at the wrong time, with no other recourse but to comply with their demands if he wanted to live.

Gideon shook his head indecisively. This kid deserved a chance at life, but what to do, put him on a horse with instruction to get as far away as possible or take him back to Fayetteville and talk to the judge. One solution would make him nothing more than a fugitive, a prime target for bounty hunters or the rest of the gang who'd for sure be gunning for him. The other option placed him on the mercy of the court, which could work in his favor if he'd tell the law the details of the gang's activities, including their identities. Given the circumstances under which he'd been taken and the short length of time he'd been with the gang it just might get him a suspended sentence.

The fire popped loudly breaking the silence causing Gideon to visibly jump, thus bringing an end to his ruminations. He was about to expound on these when the boy posed a question that brought an end to his indecision.

"Parson, the commandment says 'Thou shalt not kill'," Pinky swallowed hard before continuing, "I just broke that... I-I guess I'm bound for hell, right along with the rest of them, ain't I?"

Looking at the sky, Gideon smiled and reckoned they had a couple hours before it would be light enough to ride, so retrieving the Bible he settled down to teach the boy about God's love and forgiveness. Hopefully, with the dawning of day there'd be a new soul registered in the books of heaven. Suddenly, the water in the creek seemed to run louder; a good swift creek, just the thing for baptizing.

He stopped mid-thought, suddenly reminded that God always takes care of his children. The new convert as well as the well-seasoned servant. Immediately, a sense of peace filled his mind… the best answer for Pinky, no… no more of that name, Calvin would be the courts. After all, it wouldn't be right to encourage a child of God to become a fugitive of their land's laws when they just decided to obey God.

Chapter Eight

It was a restless congregation that noisily anticipated dismissal of the usual Sunday morning service. They were anxious to get with friends and discuss the disappearance of Harriet Collier and the new physician that had arrived in town with Doc Carter.

Their noisy surmising was somewhat hushed as Rev. Woolens turned from the pulpit, motioning for Sheriff Amos Scott to join him. Lifting his hands for silence, the minister waited patiently for total quiet before continuing.

"I know you all have a lot of questions regarding Mrs. Collier and the presence of the new physician Doc Carter's been showing around," he began.

A murmur ran through the congregation and the reverend again held up his hands for silence.

"Sheriff Scott has been looking into the disappearance of our dear sister and he asked to speak briefly while you're all here this morning to ease your worries. Meanwhile, remember to keep this lady in your prayers."

He then gave a brief nod to the sheriff and stepped aside allowing room for a wiry little man to take his place. The short lawman approached the podium; his chest puffed out like a little Bantam rooster and peered over the raised structure at the waiting parishioners with an air of self-important annoyance.

"Ahem," he cleared his throat noisily. "From all appearances it looks as though Mrs. Collier's leaving town was her own choice. It doesn't look like the two strangers that came through the other day and her disappearance are connected in any way, especially since she was last seen headed out to Olivia Cole's unaccompanied by anyone."

He paused to clear his throat once again.

"Now, I took a little ride all the way past the Cole farm and then clear up to Memphis and I didn't see hide nor hair of Mrs. Collier or her buggy or horse or anything indicating there could've been trouble, so all I can say is she just left town. However, yisterday, I received a telegram that a Pinkerton Agent is on his way here to look into this matter further. It seems the lady may be in a serious situation back where she came from."

The room buzzed as everyone, especially the shocked women, whispered and speculated about their recent companion. Raising his hands for quiet and being totally ignored, the sheriff scowled impatiently.

"BE QUIET!" he thundered, bringing an indignant silence to the crowd; then replacing his scowl with a grimace, of smug satisfaction he continued, "The Pinkerton's issued an order, Otis Brown, for you to hold off before cleaning or leasing the house she rented from you. They want to go through it. So please leave it locked up."

He was briefly interrupted as Otis voiced a questioning objection to this, but with thinly veiled patience the sheriff listened and responded, "Yes, I believe they will accommodate you for loss of revenue," he smirked.

Having satisfied the tightfisted landlord, Sheriff Scott paused before proceeding, "If any of you have information regarding Mrs. Collier and her whereabouts," his gaze swept over the crowd resting momentarily on Olivia Cole, "You're strongly encouraged to talk with me about it. No need for you to bother the Pinkerton's, since I'll be working with them," he finished boastfully.

The congregation remained quiet, but all eyes turned toward Olivia with suspicious curiosity. The woman looked around, her face blushing self-consciously before addressing the minister.

"I admit I was good friends with Harriet, but I know nothing of her whereabouts or any kind of trouble she may be in… honest, Reverend Woolens. """

"Now, Mrs. Cole," the sheriff placated, "no one means to cast any ill favor towards you. We all know you two were friends… practically bosom buddies," he grinned, "but now that don't mean nothin'."

He yawned widely and stepped back to allow the reverend to resume the podium once more. Once again, the congregation broke into restless whispers and mumblings. Reverend Woolens smiled uneasily at his flock over this last exchange.

"This is indeed a different Sunday service… one I daresay won't be repeated for a long time," he began, but brightened quickly with his next announcement. "Now, to close things with a most joyous occasion and for that I'll turn things over to Doc Carter."

Doc ambled to the front of the church and smiled jauntily at the faces before him.

"Well," he shuffled, waiting for everyone to settle down. "I've lived in this settlement that's now grown into a good-sized town all my life. And for the past twenty-five years I've taken care of everyone's births, burns, bumps, bruises, and breaks, of course with the exception of those three years I served our ill-fated South."

He stopped for a moment as though reflecting on those years before continuing.

"For the most part, it's been a real pleasure but now I'm getting older, and I'd like a little time to myself to read and go fishing… and… well, I want to get married," he paused turning, and held out his hand to a lady sitting at the far end of the front row.

Gasps from various women could be heard as a blushing Maude Sharp made her way to his side and joined hands with the smiling doctor. Turning back to face the congregation, Doc continued resolutely.

"I've carried a spark for this gal since we were kids and I finally got her to consent to marry me."

His speech was interrupted as someone from the back hollered good-naturedly, "Lordy George Carter! Did you need some lessons in sparkin' or was you waitin' till you come of age?"

The congregation burst out laughing as the doctor chuckled and responded in kind, "It took her this long to decide if I was worth it or not. Y'all know how I'm always running around the county from one woman's house to another… doctors have way too many female callers," he grinned cheekily. "This young man is about to find that out," he stated pointing to a new member of the congregation.

"Good people of Jasmine, I'd like you to meet your new physician, Dr. Andrew Meeks. He's a good man… a fine doctor, in fact he's better than I am; and if you're lucky he'll stay single and treat your ailments," he paused then grinned good-naturedly, "as long as I have. You see, it's my opinion that country doctors spend way too much time away from home to be a proper family man, which is why Ezra Stockton," he raised his voice addressing the back of the church, "I never married before now… rest assured I know all about sparkin'! Just ask my Maudie here."

Maude smacked Doc on the arm, her red cheeks giving witness to her discomfort at being on such public display. Doc grinned and squeezed her hand.

Dr. Meeks stood and addressed the crowd, indicating his pleasure in being their new physician; and reassuring everyone that he was not married, nor had prospects for getting married. This was a move he would likely regret, given his tall, good looks and the many sighs and blushes of the women present. A hearty applause from the congregation followed the doctor's announcement as he returned to his seat.

"Now," Doc Carter announced stepping forward once more, "if you have time to stick around you're cordially invited to witness the nuptials of Maude Sharp and George Carter… right now!" He winked at the congregation before continuing, "as long as it took me to get her to say yes, well … I can't afford to let her get away from me."

Everyone joined in the laughter, applauding their approval. No one noticed the Parson and young boy that slipped quietly into the back of the church and took a seat.

* * *

Empty Boot Saloon
Traders Bluff, Mississippi

Shifting uncomfortably in the hard bottomed chair, the lone man sat quietly, slouched over his mug of warm beer. Feigning a stupor, resembling someone either drunk or in bad need of sleep, he listened attentively to the conversation at the next table. It finally appeared that the Walters gang was ready to move out. The one called Cutler was as usual issuing demands along with belligerent insults, leaving no one in doubt that patience had long run out.

This vile discourse was suddenly interrupted by the loud crash of the tavern's doors smacking against the wall with an explosion of sound that dropped a foreboding hush over the occupants inside. All eyes watched as short, scruffy Harley Boroughs hurried across the room, heading straight towards Hiram Walters.

Cutler addressed the old man with a contemptuous sneer, rendering him speechless at first.

"Well, spit it out old man. You got somethin' to say or not?"

Harley took time to move the wad of tobacco he'd been chawing on to the back side of his mouth, giving him the appearance of a whiskered chipmunk, before relating how he'd just come from Jasmine and heard some man tell the undertaker to carve the name

Elam Hopper on a grave marker. A stunned silence followed this announcement as the gang members seemed to digest this somewhat uncertainly. Hiram finally spoke up to ascertain what he'd just heard.

"Are you sure of what you're sayin'… your tellin' us the truth?"

"Course, I'm tellin' the truth," the old man sputtered indignantly.

Ellis slammed his fist on the table, directing a list of expletives toward his, for once slack-jawed, leader.

"I told ya somethin' was wrong… I told ya, I heard it in my soul…told ya to let me go… Me and Hiram both said this was takin' way too long… but no, Cutler the big boss man, he-e-e gives the orders!" Ellis broke off as Hiram began to question Harley further.

"Did you see anyone else with this man… like a boy about 16 or 17 years old?"

"Naw," Harley shook his head. "I even stayed around to watch 'em put him in the ground. Sure enough, it was Elam… deader than a doornail. They said he'd been shot right through the heart."

Ellis rose and stormed out of the tavern before he did something stupid like drawdown on Cutler, which most likely would end with him joining Elam. Hiram started to follow, but then sat down. He had more questions.

"You say there was just this one man, did you get his name?"

Harley scratched his beard thoughtfully, "Naw, no name, they called him Parson though. He looked kind of like one, too, but funny thing… he wore a gun. I never seed a Parson with a gun belt on before. Have you?" he asked Hiram wonderingly.

"How long were you in Jasmine?" Hiram asked impatiently, ignoring the question. "Did ya hear any other talk… like gossip about a strange girl showin' up, or any other odd goings on there?"

"Yeah," Harley nodded and went on to tell them about the sudden marriage of the town's old sawbones.

"The whole town was talkin' about how quick like these two people up an' married; sold everything they owned an' jest left town. Seems like another one of their townsfolk had skedaddled a few days afore that. People was sure talkin' about that… you know, wonderin'."

He broke off swallowing noisily. "I tell you what, I'm gittin' a powerful thirst from all this jawin'."

He stopped again to quirk a shaggy eyebrow questioningly at his interrogator. Hiram threw a dollar on the table but held it down long enough to ask one final question.

"Did any of these people have names or is your memory to dry to recollect?" he asked sarcastically.

Harley stared longingly at the money on the table before scrunching up his eyes in concentration. At last, he burst out, "Yeah, the sawbone's name was George Carter… and that woman that left town… I think they said her name was," he thought for a moment squeezing his forehead as though the pressure would somehow cause the name to simply pop out.

Finally, he looked at Hiram, "I-I just cain't member it," he mumbled helplessly.

"Just one more question," Hiram picked up the dollar holding it out tentatively. "How many blue bellies was hangin' around Jasmine?"

The old man shook his head negatively, "None, not nary a one. The only law I saw was a sheriff, an' he don't have a deputy." He scratched his head and reached for the dollar, "Guess it's a right peaceful little town."

This time he snatched the dollar and quickly made his way to the bar. Hiram looked across the table, taken aback by Cutler's silence. He kept staring until the stunned partner looked up.

"Cain't believe the kid had it in him," he fumbled for words.

"Yeah well, I ain't all that convinced Pinky did it, but he's gotta be around somewhere up there… else how would they've known Elam's name?"

Experiencing a moment of superiority at his partner's rattled senses; Hiram rose to take advantage of the situation.

"Well, I say let's ride for Jasmine. I know Ellis has some questions about his brother, and we know Hannah was headed there, so I reckon we better disrupt this peaceful town with some questions.”

Hiram paused contemplatively, “Ya know… there's somethin' sort a suspicious about all these people suddenly leavin' town. You don't reckon our little Hannah high-tailed it away with one of these good folks do ya?”

“Yeah,” Cutler agreed resuming his normal character to lean forward eagerly. “I believe ya got somethin' there Hiram.”

He sat back, his mind working furiously, “Here's what we do. You and Ellis get the horses while I get supplies. I get a better price on goods than you or Ellis,” he grinned nastily. “We ride in thirty minutes.”

And with this announcement, their self-proclaimed leader was back to his old self.

Hiram shrugged it off, taking time to pitch money on the table for their drinks while giving his leg time to settle squarely in its prosthetic. Finally feeling somewhat secure, he moved hurriedly, bumping the table behind him hard enough to spill beer all over the arm of its occupant. The man jerked spasmodically, not bothering to look up, but instead glancing around apprehensively; as though woken from deep sleep.

Hiram gave a derisive snort and quipped unapologetically, “Lazy dog, find a bed,” with that he hurried out the tavern to find Ellis.

The barmaid came over to wipe up the spilled beer. "Not much for manners is he," she questioned watching Hiram walk away.

Turning back, she examined the stranger closely. She had been supplying this man information on the Walters gang for the past two weeks, for a hefty fee, and he'd paid whatever price she asked without hesitation.

It was obvious he was a loner, never seeking anyone's company or sitting in for a round of poker. Several patrons had asked who he was, but nobody had as yet bothered him. There was a kind of unwritten code at the Empty Boot; no questions asked, and any information forthcoming was either picked up by eavesdropping or strictly volunteered. He always ordered one beer and never finished it while either playing solitaire or pretending sleep at a table close within hearing of Hiram Walters. So far, he'd been lucky, either that or the gang was slipping; any other time they would've noticed someone hanging so close for such a long period of time.

She could tell by his manners and soft-spoken voice that he wasn't your typical river ruffian or outlaw. However, he did share one of their traits; a closed mouth, no defining information whatsoever, and even though she'd posed questions a couple of times during their exchanges the response was always a brief smile and a shrug. Glancing around at the other patron's loud discussions over the demise of one of the Walters gang, she tried again.

"What's your name?" she flirted letting her eyes travel the height of him, admiring the looks of the tall well-built man; relieved he hadn't challenged Hiram Walters to a fight.

"Nobody," the stranger mumbled non-committally. "What's yours?"

"You know my name... Sue Ellen, but people call me just Sue," she broke off under his intense stare.

"Well just Sue, I believe it's time to ride," he stated scratching a chin that showed several days growth of whiskers, "but first I need a shave." He needed to kill some time, before following the Walters gang to Jasmine.

"I'll do it for ya... for free," she grinned invitingly.

The man grinned back and tipped his hat, "Another time perhaps," he replied, handing over some coins to pay for his beer, including a generous tip for her.

Pausing momentarily, he bent down and kissed her cheek softly, "Thanks just Sue, I hope you make it out of this town."

Straightening, he headed for the door without looking back. That's the most she'd get from him 'pretty girls are just complications that slow a man down; besides she didn't have eyes like the girl back in the woods. Sue Ellen clasped her cheek and sighed longingly as the handsome man strode toward the back exit. She wouldn't mind this one staying around a little longer. Shoot, she'd wait on him for nothing, just 'cause he was so nice. Shaking her head regretfully, she watched him close the door, knowing he'd never come this way again.

"The nice ones never do," she whispered bleakly.

Chapter Nine

Jasmine, Mississippi

---

aving arrived about an hour before, the lone figure was now standing over the newest gravesite in the cemetery. The gravedigger listened surreptitiously to the mourner's sorrowful lament. Being careful to represent the appearance of his job duties, he turned over another shovel of dirt hoping no one would notice it was the same shovel full he had been moving around for the past thirty minutes.

"Elam, I heard ya call that night, I don't know how, but I heard. My soul's been cryin' ever since and," he stopped talking to wipe a bandanna across his face. "I-I feel like a part of me done shriveled up and died. I-I don't know how to get along without ya, 'cause we've been together since we's borned, but I reckon I got to go on, if for no other reason than to find that stinkin' kid and kill him. Pa always said 'eye for eye'."

The man stopped talking to take a shuddering breath and wipe his face once more.

"Elam, I guess this is the last time I'll be talkin' to ya for a while, I'm s'posed to go with Hiram and Cutler to catch Hannah. Don't worry though, I'm gonna get that Pinky… you just rest easy… us Hoppers don't take kindly to someone killin' our kin." He turned to go, then twisted back as though unable to leave his brother behind.

Catching a sob before it slipped out, he shuffled uneasily, "Elam, I ain't never told no one I loved em, not even ma, but I'll say it this one time, I love ya little brother."

The man then pulled in a long shaking breath, threw his head back and emitted a loud raspy cry that resonated with a sorrowful anger. Turning quickly, he stomped away from the cemetery.

The gravedigger watched the mourner's descent down the hill and entrance into Smithies, a rundown tavern on the outskirts of Jasmine. Purposefully taking time to return the duster and digging implements back beside the huge oak tree that shaded the graveyard, he retrieved his horse; time to grab another nasty beer.

He'd never understand white man's thirst for the vile stuff, and even though he was half white its taste had always been repulsive to him. However, it helped one blend with the crowd when your purpose was simply to listen and learn. Reining up beside the old worn building, he pulled his black Stetson a little lower over his forehead and entered Smithies.

It wasn't a large place, nor was it furnished elaborately. The bar consisted of three large barrels placed strategically apart with a flat rough plank laid across their tops for the placement of beer mugs, whiskey bottles, and elbows, while emptied vegetable cans served as spittoons. An old rundown piano sat at the back of the room where a lost looking leftover of the war plunked out "Dixie" with one finger. Good thing there weren't any blue bellies around.

Glancing towards the bar, he noticed Ellis Hopper, the mourner from the graveyard, nursing a bottle of whiskey. Knowing his own appearance bore no resemblance to the lazy drunk he'd impersonated in Traders Bluff, he stepped up to the bar to stand with his back to Ellis; just to be safe. Ordering the usual, he leaned casually on the splintered wood top and listened as the bartender divulged the events that had stirred the little community over the past weeks: the disappearance of Harriet Collier, the sudden marriage of the town's old doctor George Carter and Maude Sharp and rumors about the tall redheaded fellow that some swore was a girl.

The bartender told how Doc Carter and the Sharp woman up and sold everything they owned to take a wagon train west. He couldn't be sure, but he thought that redheaded fellow was going too. As far as that Harriet Collier was concerned, nobody knew what happened to her or where she'd gone, but the Pinkerton's were on her trail too. That last bit of information was provided with an air of amazement that the Pinkerton's would be after a woman.

He waited patiently to see if any other information was fourth coming and sure enough Ellis Hopper took a deep breath and asked about his brother's death. The bartender related how Parson Gideon Mason had brought the dead man in saying he'd found him dead in the woods, and yeah, a young boy was with him, but no, he couldn't recollect the boy's name and hadn't seen hide nor hair of him since. Reckon he left town with the parson.

Figuring these details would be shared with the others, he took a long gulp of the weak stale brew and turned to head for his hideout; barely missing a couple of blows thrown by two half-drunk farmers arguing over their mules.

Reaching his horse at the side of the tavern, he halted midway in mounting up as the backdoor to Smithies slammed shut and Ellis Hopper yelped out, "What in the Sam Hill you doin' here?"

Stepping stealthily to the corner of the building he peered around to see the other two members of the Walters gang. Liking this far better than hovering on the outskirts of their campsite, he flattened his body to the side of the building and listened.

"Sheriff's out of town and there's no blue bellies around so we came in. We're only stayin' tonight. What'd ya find out?" Cutler demanded.

As Ellis related his findings, they all agreed the tall skinny redhead had to be the girl, Hannah and most likely she traveled with either Harriet Collier or the Carters to Memphis.

"That barkeep said that Collier woman left last Saturday, but the Carters left out-a here three days ago," Ellis finished.

Everything was quiet as the gang took time to mull over Ellis' information. Momentarily, Cutler spoke up describing a plan that had Ellis' riding to Memphis come morning, while he and Hiram headed to Commerce where Capt. Farley would ferry them cross the river without alerting the boys in blue. Immediately, an argument broke out as Ellis let it be known he intended to first look for that Parson that brought Elam's body in and then he was going to hunt down Pinky and kill the worthless little mongrel.

"No you're not," Cutler insisted roughly. "All them people that left out of here for Memphis ain't that far ahead of us, so you're goin' there," he glowered. "Don't waste time checkin' hotels. Go straight to the shippin' offices for schedules and list of passengers crossin' the river. Once you find out when they're going, you're to tail them till you find out which wagon train they're takin' west. Hiram and I will be waitin' for ya at Independence. If they don't leave with a train there, we'll know to go along to St. Jo…"

Hiram broke into question, "Are you sayin' that we're gonna ride with a wagon train?" It was easy to pick up a disbelieving note in his tone.

Cutler spat out a disgusted curse, "No! We trail them at a distance and take the first sure chance we get and snatch Hannah. It ought to be easy once those wagons are out on the prairie."

"No way in Hades," Ellis objected angrily. "I'm not goin' to forget my murdered brother, forget about that rotten cur that never had sense enough to shoot anybody but Elam."

"You bloody well will if you intend to live 'cause I'll plug ya here and they can bury ya up on that hill with ya brother," Cutler growled.

The telltale sound of a pistol being cocked punctuated this statement.

Hiram used a more conciliatory tone as he persuaded Ellis to go along with the plan, promising that once they grabbed Hannah, the location and demise of Pinky would definitely take place. He knew too much about their identities and where they holed up to remain alive. The man at the side of Smithies returned soundlessly back to reenter the tavern; may as well get some directions. Then, whistling loudly and tunelessly, he returned for his horse. Reaching the animal, he mounted and headed out the road to Memphis.

Settling in for the ride, it felt good to be in the lead for a change and knowing where the gang was headed. Well, the odds of catching up to his quarry had never looked so good. The past two months of skulking around had finally paid off and the Walters gang, mainly Cutler, was within their grasp.

"Okay boy," he soothed patting his horse's neck, "let's ride, gotta get a telegram to Rhys and take a little boat ride… then, we're heading for the wide-open plains of home."

* * *

The Riverside Hotel
Memphis, Tennessee

"There," the woman sighed, laying down a box of patches containing an assortment of beauty marks similar to the one at the corner of her upper lip.

"Not bad, if I do say so myself," she remarked stepping back to carefully study her reflection.

The image in the looking glass displayed an almost pretty female of questionable age. Dressed in a style that showed off a slender waist and generous bosom, she could pass for a 20-year-old from a distance or in a carefully lighted setting. Her elaborate coiffure of strawberry blond tresses, arranged in artful twists and curls to feather coquettishly over one eye, gleamed brightly in the sunlight filtering through the lace curtain of her hotel window. However, a closer examination presented a realistic vision of a mature woman touched by the fingers of trying times, as fine lines radiated from rouged lips too often pursed. Wide blue eyes that once snapped at the world with exuberant impatience now watched warily with a hardened, calculating expression.

Still though, Delia Spencer presented an attractive, experienced companion for any unsuspecting lonely gentlemen. Her carefully practiced demure personality enhanced with a feigned air of helplessness, was the perfect lure necessary to complete the next step of her plan; catch a wealthy gullible suitor, wed quickly, and move the besotted boob west. That's what she'd planned to do in the last town, but the only available possibility there was nothing more than a smug, self-righteous saw bones.

"Humph," she exhaled disgustedly recalling the demise of her plans.

He was too busy mooning over a frumpy old spinster to appreciate a woman of quality.

"Marriage," Delia exclaimed bitterly, "a sick joke men play on women to keep us penniless, powerless, and always in the background bowing and fetching like a trained dog," she muttered remembering her earlier matrimonial attempts.

That first marriage had taken place when she was Eugenia Simpson, a precocious 17-year-old, impatient and reckless in her unconventional appetite for flirting, drinking whiskey, and gambling on everything from games of chance to horse races. The only child of Caroline and Fred Simpson grew up spoiled and hanging on her daddy's coattails as he taught her everything about Atlanta's male society, totally disregarding his wife's cries regarding propriety.

Following their early deaths resulting from a diphtheria epidemic, she became a very wealthy ward of her favorite uncle, Barclay Simpson, who promptly picked up where her daddy's tutelage had stopped. Atlanta's matrons would *'tsk, tsk'* and gossip that her reputation was overlooked only because of her family's wealth.

That first matrimonial endeavor had been with Gregory Buckner, her opposite in funding, but equal in appetites. An ever-present accomplice, this too handsome, slick talking, no account from the wrong side of the tracks, served as Eugenia's escort enabling her admittance to places society's women abhorred. His plan was to marry and gain control of her fortune. After several failed proposals, he'd finagled a way into Atlanta's Spring Cotillion, trapped Eugenia in the garden and made sure they were caught in a compromising position by enough people that only one result was possible… a wedding ceremony.

She smiled smugly at the way that one ended eleven months later. Poor lazy sap thought sure he'd live off her family's wealth while gambling and supporting every bordello in Atlanta. Too bad he wasn't as good a shot as Uncle Barclay, who welcomed the opportunity to demonstrate what happens to stupid fobs that impugn the honor of his favorite niece.

However, Uncle Barclay provided no assistance for escape from her second marriage. In fact, he felt betrayed by her behavior and the means she'd taken to rid herself of this one. Judge Albert Cooper, Chief Judge Executive of Fulton County was a trusted friend of her Uncles. He was also a lonely old widower captivated by his pal's lovely, vivacious young niece.

The Judge had prestige, power and money, and proposed marriage under the agreement that she could spend and live to her hearts content provided her activities wouldn't cause scandal. And to accompany him to social and public events, while upholding all wifely duties at home. Eugenia accepted, thinking only of the power and money that came with being Mrs. Albert Cooper. They were married in a beautiful elaborate wedding in the spring of '59 three days after her 23rd birthday.

Regrettably, marriage tricked her again. The matrimonial duties were boring, and the nuptial chamber was extremely disappointing. Her days and nights echoed with the term *a proper wife!* This drudge, along with community obligations of reigning over Atlanta's Horticultural Society, Charity Bazaars, and endless political functions lasted a little over a year before she gave in to overwhelming discontent and began looking for a way out.

Much to the expectation of Albert's grown son, Robert, she commenced spending lavish amounts on Paris fashions and other unnecessary fripperies. Her absence at societal events explained with lame excuses became common occurrences. Actually what most people knew, but wouldn't say out of respect for Judge Cooper, was she could be found at either gambling halls or racing events; places where no respectable woman would be seen. The situation culminated when she slipped away to New Orleans with a riverboat gambler and out right refused demands to come home.

Delia shuddered at the memory of Robert finding and forcing her to return home to nurse an ailing husband who suffered a stroke, 'because of you,' he'd stormed. She'd really had little choice after being threatened with life in an asylum or other deathly arrangements. As it turned out, Albert wasn't a bit more sick than she was, in fact he was quite healthy and very pleased his little ruse had worked.

She recalled his mocking laughter at her surprise in finding him waiting in that stuffy book lined study, like a schoolmaster getting ready to mete out punishment, which is just what he did. From that point on, she was forbidden to go out in public unless accompanied by his sister Margaret or himself. A strict budget was established from which she was to manage the home and purchase only essential clothing.

She was also to be the perfect amiable companion for all the Judges social occasions. These constraints were presented in the form of an agreement that she sign and comply with or face public scorn and ridicule as a penniless divorced woman. Then again that word asylum was brought up. What choice did she have especially when Uncle Barclay refused her notes and attempts to see him?

Delia felt a tear of self-pity trickle down her cheek and quickly dashed it away, angry at her own weakness. Looking up, she met her reflection in the mirror with a self-satisfied smile. She'd gotten Albert back though for all his dictatorial actions. Oh, she'd submitted long enough to make him think she had reformed. It was just too bad he hadn't insisted she learn to cook and differentiate between varying types of vegetables. How could she have forgotten there were two kinds of mushrooms and one of them was downright deadly.

Thankfully, he'd eaten all the poisonous ones before succumbing to their affects, so when everyone arrived demanding to know what happened there was no suspicious evidence available. The doctor kept glowering at her, insisting he'd been poisoned, but nothing could be found to support this. The food they'd been dining on was exactly the same. She even took bites from each plate to prove this. His liquor hadn't been tampered with… nothing could be found to substantiate the doctor's diagnosis. Still, everyone stood about, blaming her, and figuring Albert would die that night. However, he lingered on for days, with Robert or the butler keeping a constant vigil at his bedside to make sure she never got close to him again.

During this time, Robert's loathing for his young stepmother became unbearable and one afternoon in the midst of an argument he offered her $1000 to leave and never return or contact anyone in Atlanta again. After considering the options she figured why not. There was no one to go to for help, not even Uncle Barclay; at least she'd be free of Albert. Seeing this as the only way out of a wretched existence, she readily accepted the offer. Unfortunately, greed got in the way when she accidentally discovered the combination to Albert's safe. Spying several stacks of new Yankee greenbacks, she withdrew $1000 more along with a sealed bank bag containing 50 five-dollar gold pieces.

That night while Robert was in a meeting and the butler was maintaining watch at Albert's bedside, she packed a hasty valise and headed to the train depot. She didn't dare take a carriage… too easy to track. So, she walked, disguised as a forlorn looking traveler that bore little resemblance to the spirited Mrs. Albert Cooper that once reigned over the Atlanta social scene.

Instead, Harriet Collier, a name on a headstone in the cemetery in which she hid behind to keep the night patrolman from observing her getaway, boarded a train and headed north to Virginia. In a twist of fate, luck was on her side. Fort Sumter was fired on the next day and all of Atlanta was far more concerned about the existence of their newly formed Confederacy than the whereabouts of an errant wife with the morals of alley-cat.

Delia crossed to the window, shaking off the ruminations of her past. Eugenia Simpson Buckner Cooper, a.k.a. Harriet Collier was dead. She was Delia Spencer from Virginia and right now she was late for a dinner engagement with a sweet gentleman from Colorado. Carl Langston, businessman and owner of the Silver Queen Palace in Denver; a place he described as paradise to someone such as she that adorned music, gambling, and living on the precipice of chance.

Pulling back the curtain, she watched the street below, reminding herself to use more decorum and finesse on this one than she'd employed on Doc Carter back in Jasmine. It was also imperative to resist gossiping; too bad though. It was such fun to watch people squirm.

She smiled cheekily, observing the milling crowd below, "I guess it's a good thing I don't know anyone in Denver to talk about."

She felt a rush of excitement thinking of the possibility of owning something like the Silver Queen, "I'll be too busy to gossip. Because own it I will... given time."

The clock chimed five and Delia was about to let the curtain fall until something familiar caught her attention. There, on the cobbled street stood none other than George Carter and Maude Sharp. Now, what are they doing here and who is the tall woman with them – she wondered, watching the trio cross over to the Hospitality House Hotel.

"Probably that runaway Maude was harboring in her back room," she muttered drawing back as the tall girl turned and stared intently at her window.

Delia let the curtain fall in place and stepped back.

"Oh well," she shrugged, "they better watch themselves. I got a feeling the men looking for that girl are nothing to be trifled with."

Pausing before the mirror, she checked her appearance yet again. No, not a smidgen of Eugenia Simpson or Harriet Collier could be found on her anywhere. That new hair dye had done wonders covering her auburn tresses, and with the help of cosmetics... Robert Cooper, nor Maude Sharp or even the Pinkerton's would recognize her. Smiling secretively, she left the room and headed to dinner. Carl... The Silver Queen was waiting.

* * *

The crush of people in Memphis was unnerving and intimidating to someone like Hannah, who had spent the last five years cooped up in a tiny hovel with only five other people. She waited anxiously for Doc to appear with their room keys. She was hungry, tired, and done in from being bumped and jostled by hurrying strangers with no more regard for her than a sack of potatoes.

Besides, she'd felt someone watching them alight from their carriage outside the hotel in the late afternoon sun. Turning to the building across the street, Hannah stared long and hard at an observer behind the glass pane of a large-curtained window. She could tell little about them, but they were watching all the same and under her intent stare they dropped the curtain and stepped back. She could feel the hairs on the back of her neck rise in alarm. She debated whether to mention this to Maude, standing close by, but decided against it as Doc appeared with room keys in hand.

"Let's go ladies," he announced, "sanctuary at last! You can rest your weary bones; get a bath and a good meal all in the same room. Unless," he paused to watch them carefully while nodding toward a splendidly appointed area filled with well-dressed patrons, "you'd like to eat in that fancy dining room."

This hotel flaunted the most beautiful furnishings Hannah had seen since leaving her home in Oxford, with its crystal chandeliers, gilt mirrors, and highly polished lobby. Plush sofas and chairs in colors of royal blue and gold beckoned a weary traveler to rest, but it was just too open and exposed for both women whose recent years had been spent among far humbler and less crowded surroundings. Looking distressed at the prospect of eating before all those prying curious eyes, they readily voiced favor for retiring to their rooms.

Closing the door to room 216, Hannah leaned back against it sighing thankfully. At last, she was away from all the noise and strangers that made her long for the security of Maude's cozy little home. This entire day, like it's previous two, had been filled with unfamiliar people and activities, selling her jewelry, visiting the bank, and shopping for clothes. When you piled all that on someone whose exposure to what Maude called '*civilized society*' was as limited as hers, then added the sweltering heat... well, it all merged into one trying, exhausting experience.

Spying a steaming tub of water in the middle of the room, Hannah stepped away from the door and immediately began to undress, quickly jerking loose the choking ribbons that held on a hot stylish bonnet covering her still too short hair. One thing she sure didn't like about Maude's '*civilized society*' was all the clothing women had to wear simply because it was the '*proper thing to do*'. Tossing the pretty hat aside, she eagerly reached for the next article.

"I've got news for you civilized people," she muttered stripping away her shirt waist to get at the hooks of the contraption they called a corset. "It'll be snowing fireballs when I put one of these things on again," she declared flinging the offending garment across the room.

Next, she yanked off the voluminous petticoats and finally stood staring down at lacey ruffled pantaloons that reached all the way past her knees. She grimaced disgustedly knowing that tomorrow morning she'd have to put all that mass of material right back on, well, except for that corset. That thing would somehow get left behind and these drawers they called pantaloons, she vowed to cut them off above the knee. Perhaps she'd save the lace because it was so pretty but wearing something that long and hot was just too impractical she decided stripping them off.

Sinking slowly into the rapidly cooling water, Hannah leaned her head back to mull over the past three days. The trip to the jewelers had to be the most humiliating and yet rewarding task they undertook. The look on that jeweler's face as she displayed each piece registered first greed, then suspicion, and finally back to greed, once he was assured the items weren't stolen. Hannah was amazed at the final sum Doc wrangled out of the man for the entire contents $10,000… no wonder

Hiram had badgered her mother for their whereabouts.

The bank experience was much the same as the jewelers, with the manager's brusque treatment until he learned the amount of her deposit. Then, it was all smiles and *'let me help you complete papers to deposit this new-found wealth'*. Listing the account under her middle name of Elise and her father's first name, James, Hannah came away with a pass-book listing the account and $500, which she quickly hid amongst various locations on her body; leaving a minimal amount in her reticule for shopping. Doc made sure she received instructions on how to access the remaining funds from banks across the country, since they were going west.

The next venture was completed without the assistance of Doc Carter.

"The purchase of women's clothing should be left up to women," he explained and quickly took himself off to secure bookings for them on the next riverboat heading to St. Louis, the Lady Memphis.

It was a good thing Maude stayed beside her, because Hannah wouldn't have bothered with half the clothing that sales lady had insisted was necessary.

"Shoot," she puffed blowing a wet string of hair off her face. "I would have been happy with a couple pair of dungarees and shirts and a new pair of boots."

Pushing further thought aside, she quickly washed her hair, finished the bath, and rose to dry, before wrapping her body in a soft, thick cloth. Looking at the array of clothing and boxes on the bed, Hannah was glad Maude thought to purchase the small steamer trunk now sitting on the other side of the bed. Her old valise sure wouldn't hold all of this. Shoving the new things aside, she dumped her pitiful old clothes in the cleared space and stepped back to think, only to be interrupted by a soft knock at the door.

"May I come in?" Maude called quietly.

"Yes!" Hannah responded eagerly. "Maude, it's been years since I've had so much… stuff. It will take a whole day just to pack."

"Well," Maude paused reaching down to gather Hannah's old clothes, "we can get rid of these. You won't need them now."

Hannah reached out so quickly she almost dropped the towel.

"Oh no, I'm keeping my dungarees and shirts. You never know when these things will come in handy," she argued snatching the items from Maude's hands to hold them protectively. "Besides, they're a lot more comfortable to wear than all that… that get up," she finished pointing accusingly at the new clothing.

Maude relented, knowing this was a losing battle and turned to pick up the discarded carpet bag.

"This bag looks pretty roomy. I believe we can get all your old clothes in here and perhaps your riding skirts and a couple of shirt waist if we just get rid of…" Her words trailed off as she started pulling out a stiff once white voluminous garment. "What is this Hannah?" she asked while making a thorough examination of the silk and lace concoction.

"That's my mother's wedding gown from her first marriage. She wrapped her jewelry box in it before burying them. Said they were meant for my future, and I was never to bother them until the day I left Hiram's for good." She stopped speaking and looked at Maude questioningly.

"Do you think she figured I'd get away from him someday?"

"I don't know about that," Maude responded absently, "look here," she said, holding up its skirt to Hannah.

"See this gathered tuft right here… well, they're tiny pockets all around the bottom of this dress, from waist to hem, and each one contains a 20-dollar gold piece in its center. And that's not all! Just look at the sleeves and bodice," she held the sleeves up, "They're encrusted with, if my guess is right, more jewels!"

Hannah inspected the dress sleeves closely before picking up its skirt.

"How many of these…uh tufts are there?" she asked curiously.

"I haven't counted," Maude mumbled laying the dress face up on the bed. "You understand it will ruin this dress to take these things off it," Maude looked at

Hannah solemnly. "You'll not ever get to wear it," she stated.

Hannah shrugged negligently.

"Makes no never mind to me since I don't plan to marry, and besides, I'm afraid my body proportions vastly exceed my mother's. I'm about a foot taller than she was and let's just say she was little. You can tell by looking at the dress that I would never wear it, so since it's mine," she shrugged, "cut it up! It will be far easier to carry money across the country than a pile of valuable material that could easily be lost or stolen, but first, how many tufts are there?"

Maude shook her head and began counting. "My word, there's forty around the very bottom, twenty above that and ten above that."

Using Hannah's pocket-knife, she slit open the material covering each tuft to reveal a shiny twenty-dollar gold piece.

"That's $1400 just in the skirt. I have no earthly idea what the bodice is worth," she turned a bewildered look on Hannah. "Child, just how much money did your mother come from? Wait till Doc sees this."

"I don't know for sure, but it's a good thing those big skirts were in fashion," Hannah chuckled. However, her next statement quickly dispelled the lighthearted moment. "You know, I overheard the fight mother had with Hiram the night before we left Oxford, accusing him of losing her fortune. She never spoke about any of her past after that. She just told me those jewels and this gown were my future and she'd rather them rot in the dust than for Hiram to get them."

Maude shook her head sadly and hugged the forlorn looking girl standing beside her.

"Well," she straightened and gathered the wedding gown, "your mother surely did leave you a good future. I figure you and Doc are going to visit that jeweler again. Hmm, I wonder if you should take this to a different one? That one yesterday was a mite suspicious. Good thing his greed got in the way! Now, get dressed and come over to our room when you're finished. We'll pack this stuff later," she stated waving at the bed. "And cheer up young lady, we've just found out you're probably worth another little fortune," she smiled good-naturedly closing the door on her way out.

Hannah watched Maude leave, shaking her head worriedly. She'd grown fond of the Carter's, and she knew Maude felt the same about her. Unfortunately, because of this, their lives were now in danger as Hiram and Bugger would leave no stone unturned to find the whereabouts of all of them; placing Maude and Doc right the middle of their crosshairs.

"That just can't happen," Hannah whispered determinedly. "Some way, somehow I've got to protect them," she muttered recalling that even now someone was possibly watching them from across the street. She'd be sure to mention her suspicions at supper.

Picking up a camisole, she began to dress; her mind working furiously. The only solution was for them to journey separately with Maude and Doc traveling to Independence, while she went to St. Joseph. Both towns provided the means for heading west and neither of them had a fixed destination. Like what Maude said, '*We'll just wander around till we find what suits us.*' Hannah smiled at that and finished dressing.

Chapter Ten

Aboard the Lady Memphis

Hannah stood at the rail watching the river slide smoothly by thinking about all the people and sights she'd been exposed to over the last few days; far more than she'd ever imagined could possibly exist. If circumstances were different, it would've been fun to look around Memphis at all the shops and buildings; or even now to explore this boat. But there just wasn't time, besides nothing could be enjoyed when you constantly felt someone watching you; like right now, she frowned turning slightly to look over her shoulder.

Earlier, she could've sworn that Elam or Ellis, one of the two of them, was standing across the deck. She'd never been able to tell them apart, but that was neither here nor there; the fact remained that at least one of them was on board. Given the situation,

Hannah begrudgingly admitted she was glad to be wearing a dress and broad brimmed bonnet, since both articles hid her identity. The only thing the gang had ever seen her wear was boys clothes, so hopefully if one or both twins were lurking around, surely, they'd not recognize her.

Catching sight of her hands she grimaced, "well, they might know it's me if they see these," she scowled scrutinizing their work roughened condition and the jagged fingernails she'd not been able to resist chewing on.

"If I could only get used to wearing these darn things," she muttered carelessly crushing the tea gloves clutched in her left hand.

Sliding discreetly behind a tall broad-shouldered gentleman, thankfully he stood a good four or five inches above her; she cautiously peeked around his shoulder and unwittingly let out a startled audible gasp.

"Are you okay Miss?" he turned to inquire in a quiet concerned voice.

Hannah looked up into a stern, yet handsome face with a pair of the blackest eyes she'd ever seen. It felt like she could drown in them and for a moment absolutely nothing registered... no words, no utterances. Finally, her rattled senses settled down and she managed to mumble a quiet *I'm sorry*, before taking a step back and tripping on the hem of her dress.

"Here," he reached out and grasped her hand, "let me help you. How about we walk over to those chairs and have a seat. You look a bit shaken up."

Time seemed to stop for a minute or two, but at last Hannah's brain began to work.

"No, no thank you, I need to go speak with my companions. I-I'll be all right."

Pulling her hand free, she backed up quickly and offering the man a brief smile turned and slipped away, hopefully without drawing anyone else's attention. Maude and Doc had to be warned that some of the gang was aboard. Part of her was clamoring to run.

"*What if they'd already gotten to them? No, no!*" her mind screamed as she hurried around the corner.

Thankfully, the corridors weren't crowded and there was no one to notice how high she lifted her skirt to allow for big quick steps. After all, there was a time to be '*lady like*' to please this civilized society, but there was also a time to use common sense… like now! Hannah's heart pounded and her hands visibly shook as she reached out to knock on the couple's state room door. They were also empty she noticed; wondering where on earth she'd dropped those gloves.

"Oh well, there's a lot more to worry about right now than lost pieces of frippery," she snorted waiting anxiously for the door to open.

Without warning a large hand grasped her upraised arm from behind and twisted it roughly and painfully behind her back.

"What… no, NO!" she yelled loudly, purposefully wedging her foot against the doorway to stop the backward pull of being dragged away.

Dropping suddenly to her knees, she managed to trip her assailant, which sent him staggering awkwardly across the corridor, thus breaking his bruising grip on her arm. Hesitantly, dreadfully, Hannah looked up to see one of the twins getting to his feet.

"Elam… Ellis whichever of the two you are… get out of here. I'm not going anywhere with you," she spat out angrily.

Ellis grinned nastily as he leaned against the opposite wall.

"Why, Miss Hannah?" he bowed mockingly, "I don't believe I've ever seen you look so good. Hiram and Cutler would just love to see you all gussied up like this."

He let out a sinister cackle. "My, my, my, if you ain't a pretty sight. I knowed it was ya the minute I spied that little piece of red hair sticking out. I says to myself… Ellis ain't nobody got hair that red 'cept for Hannah Walters."

"You know that's not my name," she hissed furiously. "He never legally adopted me, so my last name is the same as always… Todd. Not that it matters now though, I turned 18 last week."

Ellis looked thoughtful for a moment and then shrugged negligently, "Makes no difference; you're still comin' with me," he said moving toward the state room door she had previously knocked on. "See, I know you're travelin' with the Carters and they're right here behind this door. Now, ya got a choice… Come with me quite like and when we get off this boat we'll hightail it to the gang or… ya can raise a ruckus and I'll just go in and shoot the newlyweds and tell everyone you did it. It's your choice."

Hannah watched Ellis anxiously, knowing he was fully capable of carrying out his threat. Her mind raced through several scenarios to come up with a way out of this situation without anyone getting shot, leastways she and her companions. Catching movement behind Ellis she noticed the man from the deck who had offered his help. He crept stealthily closer to Ellis, nodding for her to continue, so taking a deep exaggerated breath; she stood straight and nodded to her abductor.

"Okay Ellis, we'll do it your way, but first let me go in and get my valise and reticule. I'll need the money I got for selling the jewels." Receiving a knowing grin and nod, she turned to knock briefly on the door before calling out, "it's me… Hannah. I'm coming in."

Having her back turned, Hannah never knew how things started, but upon hearing a loud smack and a heavy groan, she spun around to see the man from the deck and Ellis fighting furiously. Knowing Ellis to be a dirty fighter, she waited for the moment when the two were close enough and reached down to pull his pistol smoothly from the holster tied to his leg.

Startled, Ellis whipped around and let go a hard right punch, catching the unprepared young woman smack in the eye and forehead, causing her head to jerk backwards and collide with the metal doorjamb. Hannah stood momentarily stunned, before crumpling senseless to the floor.

Much later, she came to lying on a bunk and looked up into three worried faces. Blinking rapidly, she tried to concentrate on each one, but didn't have much success. The images kept wavering in and out of focus. Her attempt to rise was also a dismal failure as she quickly laid back to give the room time to stop spinning.

"Wh-what happened out there?" she asked hesitantly. "Where… Where did Ellis get to? I-I told you we were being followed," she complained. "Now, you see Maude, now you see why we have to travel separately," she asked urgently.

Maude reached down and pushed her hair back. "Calm down Hannah, you've got quite a bump on your head. Doc says you need to stay quiet and rest for a spell. We'll talk about that later."

"No, we need to talk now," Hannah argued adamantly. "By the way, where did Ellis go?" she asked.

"You don't have to worry about him anymore," her rescuer said through clenched teeth while nursing a busted lip. "Someone must've alerted the ship's captain, because he came barreling around the corner yelling for us to stop. Upon spying him, Ellis ran and when I gave chase, he jumped overboard."

Hannah watched the handsome stranger talk, again somewhat mesmerized. He stood at least 6'4" and the breadth of his shoulders and solid build made even her feel undersized. But it wasn't his handsome visage that drew her; it was those unfathomable dark eyes coupled with his calm self-assured dignity. Strangely, she felt compelled to rely on him.

Shaking a pain racked head, Hannah snapped to her senses. That bump must have addled her mind. Hadn't she just escaped from five years of living among five men and not a one of them trustworthy? And weren't they all after only one thing from women… like those two that stole Samson?

This one might be handsome and has nice manners, but given the right dressings couldn't they all carry out some semblance of chivalry… hadn't Hiram tricked her mother like this? Besides, what would this man think upon learning she'd lived all those years alone with five outlaws? Oh no, he has to go she decided, rising to sit gingerly on the side of the bed as the man continued.

"Judging from his reaction, I'd say this Ellis never paid for his passage, but simply came on board with everyone else, and managed to avoid stewards and other officials."

The stranger stopped talking and seemed to ponder briefly before asking, "Now, I know why this man is after you. May I be of help?"

Hannah spoke up quickly, "How do you know anything about my situation? I've never seen you before." Hannah watched her rescuer warily and waited.

"I've heard talk about you for the past few weeks. You see, I've been trailing the Walters gang and ran upon them in Traders Bluff. So, I know all about your escape and the goings-on with the rest of the gang. I'm on my way to Independence to meet my partner and continue to pursue this Cutler… guy. It's a long story and I'd be more than happy to talk with you about it over supper. Perhaps we can help each other."

Hannah regarded the man warily. He might be handsome and appear reliable, but trusting others didn't come easily, especially men and besides as dizzy as she felt right now, she wasn't about to trust her own judgment either.

"Um, thank you, thank you kindly for all your help, but we'll be okay… especially since that man isn't on the boat anymore. We're headed to St. Louis and once there we can alert the authorities. So… so we'll be fine. Won't we?" she looked from Maude to Doc silently imploring their agreement.

Doc remained silent, but Maude sensed Hannah's insecurity and crossing to the tall man gently took his elbow and began walking towards the door.

"We'll be fine," she smiled patting his arm encouragingly. "As soon as this boat docks, we'll go straight to the authorities and report this man. Don't you worry; Doc and I are going to take good care of our Hannah. She's the daughter I never had, and I'm not about to lose her."

Opening the door, Maude stepped back to allow the man room to move forward, "I'm mighty beholding to you for stepping in, but now I'm sure you've got things of your own to worry about. We'll be fine," she smiled.

The stranger accepted these words quietly.

He turned and gave Hannah a long thoughtful stare, then nodded briefly before saying, "My name is Justin Findlay and I'm in room 20 on the deck below. Should you need any more help just get word to me and I'll find you."

He seemed to want to say something else but stopped and walked out.

Maude closed the door softly and Doc turned an accusing glare on Hannah.

"Why, why didn't you accept his help? We could use a nice strong man like him. Don't tell me you think we're going to fight this gang all by ourselves?" he hammered relentlessly.

Hannah realized Maude had remained quiet and let Doc carry on. Perhaps she was wondering the same thing. Looking up beseechingly at the only two people she'd cared about in a long time, Hannah pleaded.

"Don't you see Doc, I'm like some kind of incurable sickness and everyone who comes in contact with me is in danger of dying. Even that Harriet Collier probably left town so fast because they threatened her. So far, you three are the only ones I'm responsible for and my conscience can't make allowances for one more person. I never meant to involve anyone else in this… this attempt to get away. I knew the consequences… what would happen to anyone who helps me. Unfortunately, I wasn't in any condition to warn you away Doc, so here we be."

Hannah stopped to take a slow deep breath before continuing, "You can't imagine how guilty I feel because you two are so involved. Don't you realize one or both of you could end up dead? That's why I can't involve anyone else; and that's exactly why we're going to separate when we get across this river. You'll be safe among several people on a wagon train… headed somewhere to a part of the country where no one's ever heard of me. I'll be safe on a different train, traveling among a crowd, but still alone. No one will know who I am, where I'm from or anything about me. Don't you see, it's the only way?" Hannah pleaded.

She watched her companions closely, aware that Maude was ready to argue the situation. However, the ever-practical Doc coaxed his new wife gently, urging her to at least acknowledge the sense of Hannah's plan.

Finally, with tear-filled eyes Maude conceded, but not until Hannah promised they could write each other under assumed names.

Rising slowly, Hannah crossed to embrace her tearful benefactor in a warm hug.

"Now," she said pulling back to wipe her own eyes, "no more arguments; Ellis is no longer on this boat so let's enjoy the time we have left."

* * *

The man walking away from the crowded state room was certain there was more going on with the three people he had just left than what was actually being said. He got the feeling the older couple would have welcomed help, but that girl, Hannah, had been so against it. '*Why?*' he wondered. And why had he revealed his full white man name? That was something he never did!

"Addlepated sap," he smirked. "But that girl has the same sky stone eyes as the one I came across in the woods."

Reaching into his pocket for a room key, his fingers touched the gloves he'd intended to return. He didn't turn back though. They'd provide a legitimate excuse to see her again before reaching St. Louis.

What was it about this girl that stirred his blood so? Those sky-blue eyes, her lips that reminded him of plump wild strawberries? Or her fierce spirit that seemed determined to battle life alone? Was this even the same girl? Whatever it was, he better get himself under control before seeing her again. No telling what he'd blurt out the next time they met.

"Justin Findlay," he scoffed.

He hadn't used that name since leaving the care of John and Anna Montclair to live with his Cheyenne grandfather and his people at age six. He laughed again at his unconscious effort to hide that Indian part of him. All anyone had to do was take in his dark eyes, high cheekbones, and reddish tan skin to realize he carried Indian blood; after that it didn't matter if you were one fourth, one half or a smidgen… if you exhibited those features, by gosh you were a dirty Indian or savage depending on their level of hatred for anyone of Indian descent. Well, he was one half of both.

His father, Lachlan Findlay, was a tall dark man of Scottish descent who came to America as part of a French exploratory expedition and became captivated by a vast wild land where adventure abounded. He one day rescued a Cheyenne Indian woman from a bear trap she'd stepped on. Small Cloud's tribe was on the move to their wintering grounds and had no time to treat an injury.

Reaching an agreement with the chief's trapper friend, Tall Bear, the Indians adopted name for his father, the maiden's father left her in his care until the next spring. However, romance bloomed, and Justin was the product. Life was wonderful until Small Cloud contacted smallpox and died right after her baby's second birthday. Overcome with grief and loneliness his father left him in the care of the Montclair's, a couple who maintained a trading post close to the Cheyenne summer ground and returned to Scotland.

He left his son no money and four familial features to carry through life. First, a head full of wavy hair that curled far too tightly if cut short in the white man's fashion. So, he left it long enough to braid and keep hidden under a hat. Second, a loving English-speaking couple to teach him the white man's language and ways at an early age. The third item was his height, which topped off at 6'4" and lastly his name, name, which Justin eagerly traded for the Indian name of Cloud Walker upon rejoining his mother's tribe. He'd shortened this to Walker after returning to live in his father's world twelve years ago.

"Good gosh," he muttered disgustingly entering the room… pausing momentarily, as a sense of smothering washed over him.

This occurred every time he entered the cabin's close confining walls. Rhys, his partner and longtime friend, sure better appreciate the sacrifices he'd made to gather the information he was taking back. Because this was his last time ever to be on the eastern side of the Mississippi; too many buildings, too many people, and too many small airless places such as this state room.

Sighing longingly, Walker pictured the wide-open plains and his horse waiting for a good gallop. If he closed his eyes, he could see it, feel the sun and the wind, and hear the rustle of the prairie grass and the cry of a red tail hawk as it soared the skies searching for a prey. Still though his recollections were interrupted by the sky stone eyes of a pretty girl... Hannah.

Realizing that oppressive sensation had faded, Walker shut the cabin door and winced at the pain emanating from his right hand. A close examination revealed several swollen bleeding knuckles that would probably bruise by morning. He shrugged negligently, just minor inconveniences from a skirmish worth getting into, he grinned, reliving punch for punch. He'd always been a good scrapper using his height and long arms and legs to defeat his shorter Indian brothers. So far, the only man who had come near defeating him was his friend Rhys and that battle had ended in a draw due to sheer exhaustion.

"Well, today wouldn't have ended like that," Walker muttered narrowing his eyes to concentrate on the curses and parting words Ellis yelled before diving overboard.

"Go ahead half breed make a fool of yourself over Hiram Walters' woman. Just don't get attached and don't get in the way; her life's spoken for clear to its soon to be sorry end."

Recalling these words, understanding suddenly dawned… Hannah may be more attached to this gang than just the girl sleeping in the woods fleeing for her life.

"If only I'd known," he groaned.

That was the Hannah he'd sat in the Empty Boot Tavern and heard them revile and promise hellish retribution. How could someone as young as her be connected with the very gang and that culprit he and Rhys had been after for the past five years?

He prowled the small state room restlessly, his mind working to come up with reasons a young girl like Hannah could be associated with outlaws like the Walters gang. All types of connections were possible… daughter, sister, wife, or maybe someone they'd abducted… but whatever the link it sounded like the continuation of her future was definitely questionable.

Shaking his head worriedly, Walker figured Rhys wasn't going to like the plan he was coming up with, but he'd go along with it. It was the only way to keep track of Hannah and nab Rhys' target at the same time. One thing was sure, upon reaching St. Louis, he would wire Rhys again and demand they meet in Independence because their plans had just gotten a lot more complicated. Walker knew that, with or without Rhys's help, he fully intended to see that no harm came to Hannah.

* * *

Ellis clamped shivering arms tightly around the log he was holding onto, cursing his luck, as it carried him further away from his assigned duty. Cutler was going to be livid if he couldn't somehow find a way to fix this.

"Cutler can go to the devil right now," he muttered realizing the necessity to get out of the bone chilling cold water or he'd be joining Elam in the hereafter real soon… *too soon*!

Ellis shook his head forlornly as numerous regrets filled his mind; like why he hadn't put up more of a fight to go with Elam, or why he'd gambled and lost the money for ships passage,

"Or why I never learned to swim?" he hollered loudly before remembering the swampy bayous of Louisiana full of alligators and water snakes.

Okay, that one was excusable he allowed; a body didn't even wade in those murky depths, much less swim. He breathed a sigh of relief that the Mississippi didn't have alligators. It probably had some snakes… like water moccasins. He shuddered pulling as much of his body upon the log as possible.

"I'll probably freeze to death before anything else happens," he cringed as a cold wind plastered waterlogged clothing to his shivering body.

Trying his best to stay awake, Ellis thought about how close he'd come to carrying out his great plan. It had seemed so easy to simply hold Hannah and the Carters at gunpoint until they docked in St. Louis tomorrow... then not wanting her friends killed... Hannah would have willingly gone with him. Cutler and Hiram would have been satisfied.

"And I could have gone after that rotten cur Pinky... worthless little..." The words faded away as he slowly gave in to the lethargy that was gradually stealing his conscious effort to stay awake and maintain a tight grip on the log, but this battle was soon lost, and his grip slowly loosened.

Ellis suddenly jerked awake sputtering and thrashing wildly about as a strong arm clamped tightly around his upper body.

"Here, stop that," a man's voice demanded. "You're going to drown us both. Can't you tell I'm trying to fish you out of this cold water... now, hold still till I can get you on my raft."

Ellis quieted all movements as the man towed him to a sturdy raft moored securely to a large tree on the riverbank. Once there, both men struggled, but managed to hoist their water-soaked bodies aboard while coughing, gasping, and finally gulping deep breaths of air to stabilize their winded conditions. At last, the man extended his hand offering a friendly greeting.

"Name's George Napier," he panted. "Saw you slide off that log in the cold water and knew you'd be a goner if I didn't get there fast enough. Good thing I'm a strong swimmer!"

"Yeah," Ellis agreed shaking his head. "Good thing you came along," he admitted not bothering to give his name or thank his rescuer. "Where're you headed?" he asked looking around curiously at the contents of the raft.

"Memphis," George replied holding out a heavy quilt. "I don't have any dry clothes, but you can wrap up in this and at least keep the wind off. I don't want to light a fire here at this part of the river, it would likely make us a target of the river pirates that troll this area," he finished disgustedly.

Wrapping his own body in a second quilt he asked offhandedly, "How did you happen to be floating in that cold water?"

"Oh, I was aboard the Lady Memphis headed to St. Louis and somehow got shoved overboard… people was packed like sardines on that boat. I reckon nobody even know'd I was gone; leastways nobody tried to rescue me."

"I see… a little bad luck…huh?" George responded seemingly distracted.

Ellis grunted his agreement while trying to think of some way to avoid going all the way back to Memphis.

"Get some sleep if you can," George called out. "When morning comes, we'll shove off and I'll let you steer. Then, perhaps I can catch a little shut eye. I usually don't sleep much on these trips; too busy either steering or watching out for thieves." He yawned widely, "For now though, I'll keep watch till daybreak."

Too cold and exhausted to respond, Ellis lay down and was soon lulled into a sound sleep by the gentle swells of the water that lifted and rocked the raft. He awoke just as the dawn sky was emitting enough light to see by and nature's alarm clocks were going off in a cacophony of caws and whistles. Somewhere along the river bank a rooster crowed.

He lay quietly listening to the morning unfold while glancing over various objects lying around the raft. Spying a heavy crowbar propped about two feet away, he suddenly came up with a plan for getting off the river. Reaching out, he quickly pulled it inside his quilt, taking pains to make no noise that would attract attention.

Noticing his companion slumped asleep over the river craft's tiller, Ellis rose and cautiously approached from behind. Soundlessly, he lifted the crowbar over his head and brought it down on the back of the man's skull. Standing perfectly still, Ellis waited before prodding the unconscious man to make sure he was definitely out.

Feeling the raft lift, fall, and bump vigorously into the tree it was moored to, Ellis hopped off to pull it further inland. He watched his unconscious victim for any movement and seeing none, climbed carefully back on board. Moving quietly, he made fast work of rummaging through the man's belongings; scattering items haphazardly around until he at last found what he had hoped for… a cash box full of money. He stuffed it all in his pockets, but then had second thoughts. After all, the man did save his life... so what of it. Hadn't he been expecting river pirates? Good thing Cutler wasn't here, he would have cut the man's throat.

"I'm leaving your life in exchange for mine," Ellis muttered stepping off the raft.

Glancing around, he swiftly ascertained his bearings and headed north, toward St. Louis. It shouldn't take long, provided he hadn't floated too far down the river. Hopefully, there would be a town, farm, or somewhere to get a horse; after all he'd heard that rooster, which surely indicated a barnyard close by. Keeping this in mind Ellis walked swiftly watching for predators and planning what he was going to say to Cutler and Hiram. If he could make good time, they'd never have to know about his screw-up. Now that would be a first – yep, it would sure be a first.

* * *

Aboard the Lady Memphis

Hannah and Maude stepped back from a gripping hug that left both women with tear filled eyes and a bereft sense of emptiness. They'd grown extremely fond of each other over the past month and a half.

"I don't want to leave you like this. You're too young to be on your own facing the danger you're in," Maude stated being the first to break the silence. "Why can't we just go to the authorities and tell them everything now that you're of age? Surely, you're not afraid they'll still try to make you go back with that man."

"Maude, you're the closest thing to a real mother I've had since being separated from my Nana Ollie when Hiram took us from Oxford and I don't want to part any more than you," Hannah paused to wipe her eyes, "but this Walters gang has eluded the law for years and even though wanted posters on them have been posted, they've never come close to being caught. I've even heard them brag about buying off judges and law officers or finding other ways to shut them up."

She stopped talking to let those words sink in before continuing.

"I'm not willing to take that chance, especially in a part of the country where we... you and doc don't know anybody... yet. Don't you see with a wagon train you'll make friends quickly, especially with your willingness to help others and doc... well, being a doctor. People will be glad to protect you, if it comes to that, but that gang will be trailing me... so you and doc should be okay."

Watching her companion close, Hannah pushed her final chilling argument.

"If I'm with you, it will just bring trouble to the wagon train and they would probably put us off to fend for ourselves, especially once Cutler kills a few people to show the gang will do whatever it takes to get what they want."

"Okay, okay," Maude gave in with a trembling breath. "You win, but I don't like it. I'll be praying for you every mile of the way. I still wish we had let that nice young man help us. He sure was smitten with you," she finished watching Hannah blush. "Maybe you like him too," she teased.

Hannah busied herself by pulling out paper and pencil, "don't start that. I'll admit he was handsome, and I finally met a man taller than me, but that's as far as it goes. Now, I decided you can write to me using the name Jane Jackson in care of General Delivery Denver Colorado. I aim to make it that far before the snows fall... leastways before I die."

Maude took down the information with a stern reminder, "If I don't hear from you by winter..." she looked up from writing once again on the verge of tears. "It all sounds so final. You going one way, and me another. I meant what I told that man about you being the daughter I never had. It's breaking my heart to let you go. Promise me you won't take chances," she sniffed before continuing, "and you won't kill anyone if you don't absolutely have to... and if you get a chance, find a good preacher and talk to him about the Lord Jesus and saving your soul. In fact, do that as soon as possible... in case... in case something happens to you, please. I'd like to know that I'll at least see you in heaven someday."

Hannah was wiping tears again as she fervently promised to comply with all Maude's wishes. Her next words were interrupted as doc knocked loudly and entered the room whistling Camp Town Races.

"Just what I thought I'd find, two watering buckets leaking all over the place ready to flood the boat. Come on ladies, we're setting out on the adventures of our lives. And yes, there'll be challenges and dangers, but I've never known two more fierce women that are more than capable to brave the storms."

He paused for a moment to stare gravely at Hannah. "Young woman, I'm not trying to make light of the situation we're all in, especially you. I know I haven't always been the kindest to you, but... You're welcome to travel with us. We can see this thing through."

Maude's hopeful sigh was abruptly dashed when Hannah responded with a firm negative shake of her head.

"No, we've been all through this. I started this journey alone with no intentions to involve anyone else." She stood straight and looked both her companions in the eye before stating gravely, "I know what's before me and I'm ready to get on with it."

Doc reached out and patted her shoulder, stating with gruff affection, "I have the greatest respect for you and what you're trying to do for yourself... and, well... I'll always be grateful to you for bringing Maudie and me together."

He grinned impishly, "At the rate we were going… well," he winked at Maude, "we might have come together by this time oh, say… in the next two or three years provided my bride here and Harriet Collier quit fighting over me long enough to decide which one would finally get me. After all, I'm quite a prize!"

"Land sakes, George Carter," Maude exclaimed. "I don't know what to think about you," she finished shaking her head ruefully before joining Hannah in an explosion of laughter.

Doc stood frowning, looking from one to the other with a pretended air of injured pride. "Well, it's abundantly clear now, you two females have no more regard for me than that old hound dog Maude gave to the Wilkins boy. Maybe I should have taken my chance with Harriet," he huffed.

This made the women laugh harder than ever.

Shaking his head forlornly, Doc shrugged his shoulders then announced, "At least I cleared up the water buckets," which sobered his companions instantly.

At that moment, a shrill whistle sounded throughout the boat and it shook and vibrated convulsively while sliding into harbor. Not another word was said as doc and Maude embraced Hannah warmly before gathering their bags. Hannah grabbed the strap of her old carpetbag and walked hand-in-hand with Maude to the door.

"I'll have a word of prayer," Maude declared and allowing no time for objections she began. "Dear Lord, you are a gracious and Almighty God, and you know our comings and goings and even our thoughts long before we do. You are fully aware of the situation we three are in and the dangers before us on this journey to find somewhere to live in peace and do your work till you one day call us home. Resting on these assurances, Almighty God, we ask for protection from danger, your enlightenment at opportunities that may arise for help and direction, and your comforting presence at all times, and especially when our journey pass through valleys with shadows of death. And may we all wander back together someday… soon Lord… real soon," she whispered before finishing, "We ask this in Jesus' name, Amen."

Hannah opened her eyes to watch Doc and Maude hurry out the door. Panic set in and she almost called them back and agree to go with them; for right now, she felt more alone and scared than ever before. However, a forceful stiffening of her backbone and attitude aided the gripping panic to fade into a guarded fear. Asserting a severe conscious effort, she stood as though rooted to the floor unable to move, which only allowed that fear along with all the unanswered questions concerning the future to overwhelm her.

A loud knock pounded on the door across the corridor followed by a stern voice calling, "All ashore that's going ashore."

Realizing she needed to get a move on, Hannah took a deep breath and hurried out of the room to the deck below. Stopping momentarily at the river boats railing, her eyes greedily searched the disembarking passengers on the ground till she spotted her two companions. She watched until they disappeared inside a coach and sped away before turning to leave the boat and begin her own journey.

Taking a resolute step toward the gang plank, Hannah once again felt someone watching her and looked up to meet the eyes of the man called Justin Findlay. He approached her with long strides that covered the distance quickly. Maintaining a firm determined demeanor, he paused to examine the girl who had haunted his dreams for weeks. A brief smile hovered around the corners of his mouth and his eyes finally settled on hers.

Once again, Hannah was taken aback by the sheer brevity of this tall, broad-shouldered man and pulled in a deep breath just to soothe her nerves. However, the minute she looked into the depths of his deep dark eyes the nerves began clamoring all over again and she felt sure he could read every secret her soul possessed.

She jumped at the sound of a rich resonant voice as he held out an article that he was trying to give her. Mentally shaking herself Hannah snapped out of her uncommon stupor to realize he was trying to return the tea gloves she had dropped at their first meeting. Reaching out, she accepted the gloves which he pulled back temporarily to get her attention.

Looking up with a puzzled expression she at last heard what he was saying.

"Miss Todd, I know you're in trouble and I know who you're running from. I'd like to help you. I've been trailing the Walters gang for months and believe me one lone girl doesn't stand a chance against these men."

Hannah felt her temper flare at being told she didn't stand a chance, but then quickly tempered that anger. After all, he was right or he would be right if she planned on going after them, but she planned on running from them as far away as remotely possible. Clearing her throat, she looked up, only this time avoiding eye contact.

"How..." she began her voice cracking, taking a deep breath she tried again. "How do you know my name? I don't remember telling you."

He smiled again, only this time it crinkled the corners of his eyes adding charm to his already handsome visage.

"Your companions told me, but that was all they said. They were very loyal to you. Look, I've been hearing about you for the past month and the Walters gang is not going to leave you alone."

"Stop," Hannah broke in immediately.

What must he think of her if he'd been listening to Hiram and the gang talk? She felt her face flush red at guessing what he must think. She could just imagine some of the remarks that Hiram often took the liberty to say. Oh no, she had to get away from here. Reaching out, she jerked her glove from his hand and turned to descend the boat. It all happened so fast and unexpected that Justin didn't have time to counteract her actions, but he did manage to catch the words she flung over her shoulder.

"Honestly, I appreciate the offer, but this is something I have to do alone. I can't bear the thought of another person being killed because of me."

He stood silently watching Hannah hurry away; his mind set... sure as the sun rises in the east, he'd be seeing her again.

Hannah reached the station house from which to hire a coach and stopped to make arrangements. She could still sense those eyes watching her and turned around to glance back at the boat. Sure enough, Mr. Findlay was still there watching her. He held up something white and looking down she realized she'd only managed to get one glove.

Shrugging negligently, she brushed her embarrassment aside. "Oh well, another person I'll never see again," she muttered.

However, she couldn't resist letting her thoughts wander back to their earlier meeting.

Neither could she resist looking back one last time; he was still watching her.

"Hmm," Hannah walked away wondering how long she'd see and feel those eyes following her; knowing full well they'd be a compellingly presence in her dreams for many nights to come.

Fini

Biography

Hello readers,

Reading for me has always been an escape and a way to visit other countries, other times, and even become someone other than myself as I became absorbed into the characters and their stories. A book has always been my constant companion throughout the years. Due to an unfortunate accident, I became a C4-5 quadriplegic at the age of 15. My life changed in so many ways, but while curbing my physical independence, it greatly enhanced my opportunities for educational, cultural, and personal growth experiences. I have two degrees from the University of Kentucky and have been married to the most wonderful man for the past thirty-four years. We currently reside in a little town in Kentucky with our German Shepherd, Sophie.

I have read countless novels of various genres throughout the years and always wanted to write one. Well, I finally did it and

I hope it meets with your approval. This is my first attempt at such a daunting endeavor and now that I've got my feet wet so to speak, it's certainly not the last. I hope you have enjoyed reading Part One of The Wanderers: A Trail to Somewhere. Look for The Wanderers Part 2: The Perilous Trail to be out in fall 2022.